HAR
AND THE Fire Star

CERRIE BURNELL

Illustrated by Laura Ellen Anderson

SCHOLASTIC

Once there was a girl called Harper who had a rare musical gift. She heard songs on the wind, rhythms on the rain and hope in the beat of a butterfly's wing. Harper could play every instrument she ever picked up, without learning a single note. But sometimes late at night, alone with her cat, Midnight, Harper dreamed of the cloudian, an instrument sewn from silver-lined clouds, and she wondered where its magic might lead her.

Chapter One
A MIST OF MARVELS AND MYSTERY

High in the City of Clouds, on the fourteenth floor of the Tall Apartment Block, Harper was dreaming of snow. It was a dream of a gleaming whiteness that stole every sound from the world and covered the streets in silence. Not even a drop of rain could be heard. Then suddenly, through Harper's dream came a slow, rumbling purr.

She blinked a sea-grey eye open and saw her precious cat nuzzling up to her face. "Good morning, Midnight," she yawned, then Harper sat bolt upright in bed, her ears searching for sounds. But there was nothing. No patter of raindrops, no rickety trams, no splashing puddles. It was just like the quiet of her dream.

Harper darted to the window and pulled back the velveteen curtains. A bright glow swept into the room, making her blink. The entire city was coated in a sleek white mist, as strange and lovely as winter.

"No wonder I dreamed of snow," Harper smiled, scooping Midnight up so he could

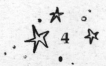

see too. "It's a mist of marvels and mystery," she whispered, her heart beginning to skip, for a mist like this could only mean one thing: the Circus of Dreams was in town!

Harper set Midnight down, seized her small golden harp and plucked three sharp notes – the secret signal to summon her friends. Then she

dashed into the kitchen, pulling on her clothes and grabbing her beautiful Scarlet Umbrella.

Ten minutes later, Harper's little kitchen was a muddle of excitement and instruments, as her friends from the Tall Apartment Block piled in. There was Nate Nathanielson, a boy who only saw darkness or light, and had a majestic wolf at his side. Ferdie, a boy with a serious scarf and serious love of poetry. His younger sister, Liesel, a girl with bright eyes and hair so tangled it was home to a dove. Isabella Lucas from the seventh floor. And whirling around in the middle of the kitchen was Harper's Great Aunt Sassy, who she lived with.

When everyone had a warm cup of lavender syrup, Great Aunt Sassy brandished her purple umbrella, almost knocking Ferdie over, and hushed everyone. Harper gulped away a giggle and stood up tall.

"The Circus of Dreams is here again!" she breathed.

A gleeful cheer went up from her friends, for they'd all visited the Circus of Dreams: a flock of floating tents held

in the air by magic, the very place where Harper had been born.

"Harper, you'll get to see your parents," beamed Isabella, swinging her into a hug.

A warm glow seemed to fill the kitchen, and Harper felt quivery with happiness. But one little thought still nagged at her, like a single snowflake on a warm summer's day.

"What shall I do?" she whispered to Midnight. He meowed gently, his green eyes glittering like two tiny emeralds, and gave Harper a wink. Carefully, she opened her Scarlet Umbrella and floated towards the ceiling. "There's something else we need to do," Harper explained as everyone turned to gaze at her.

Nate, who had been listening quietly, gave a gleaming smile and said brightly, "We've got to help the Wild Conductor win back his place in the circus."

Harper nodded and a chorus of agreement echoed through the kitchen. "You're right, my darling girl," cooed Great Aunt Sassy, swigging her lavender syrup. "Why don't you children go to the circus and I will organize an evening meeting on the rooftop at seven o'clock sharp!"

In a rush of laughter and scampering feet, the children grabbed their instruments, clattered down the stairwells and out into the City of Clouds.

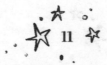

The streets were cloaked in swirls of white mist, which clung to them like cloud dust, and blotted out the street signs. But Nate was a boy who had many skills, and one of them was finding his way through the dark as easily as if it were daylight. This was really no different. As he and Smoke moved through the city he played a tune on the harmonica, so his friends could hear and follow the way. Liesel, who had been practising, picked up the melody on her shining violin. Ferdie joined on his ever-faithful button accordion and Isabella clicked a set of castanets, while Harper added harmonies on her piccolo flute.

Then they came upon a sight that stole their breath away: the red and gold stripes of a circus tent, hovering high in the air, a rope ladder trailing down to the ground just waiting for them to climb.

Isabella, who had never been to the Circus of Dreams before, squeezed Harper's hand. "It really is magical," she gasped.

"Yes," Harper smiled, "it really is," and she placed her foot on the first rung of the ladder, climbing up towards a flock of flying tents which felt like home.

Chapter Two
THE CIRCUS OF SECRETS

Inside the red and gold tent, the children found their old friend the lightning-leader waiting for them. Blue lightning crackled in her hair, making her look like a wild storm. She pulled aside the curtains at the back of the tent and, with a sly wink, ushered them through.

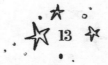

The five friends gazed at a city of brightly coloured tents pitched upon solid clouds. The umbrellas that held the clouds in the air had been disguised to look like hot-air balloons. But the children knew that this was a circus of secrets and magic – not hot air.

"Which way do we go?" murmured Isabella, staring at the many little spun-sugar bridges that linked the tents together.

"Wherever you like!" squealed Liesel, hurrying off to find her friend Rat – a boy with rodent's teeth and a troupe of dazzling rat dancers.

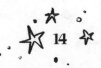

Ferdie decided to visit Faydra the fortune-teller and find out if he really was going to become a world-famous poet after all. Smoke at once began nuzzling Nate towards a tent holding an entire chocolate forest.

Harper took Isabella's hand. "Come with me and I'll show you my favourite tents," she said, giving Isabella a knowing look.

You see, Harper was the only child ever to have escaped from the Circus of Dreams and the clutches of Othello Grande, the ringmaster. Her parents had managed to smuggle her out on the night of the fearsome storm. So whenever Harper visited the circus, she had to pretend to be an ordinary girl enchanted by its many wonders.

Harper led Isabella through the doorway

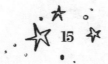

of a tent that smelled like Paris. Inside she found a bakery not quite like any other. Isabella marvelled at a jar of jellied fish that actually seemed to be swimming. She giggled at a display of sugar-plum ballerinas who twirled of their own accord. But what made her smile the most was the sight of Harper hugging Hugo the extraordinary baker – who was in fact her father.

Hugo gave both of them stacks of cakes and treats. Harper was used to all the glorious flavours, particularly the tea that tasted of memories, but Isabella was spellbound. She found herself wishing that she could stay there for ever, tasting a different cake every day.

Next they visited a tent of mystical

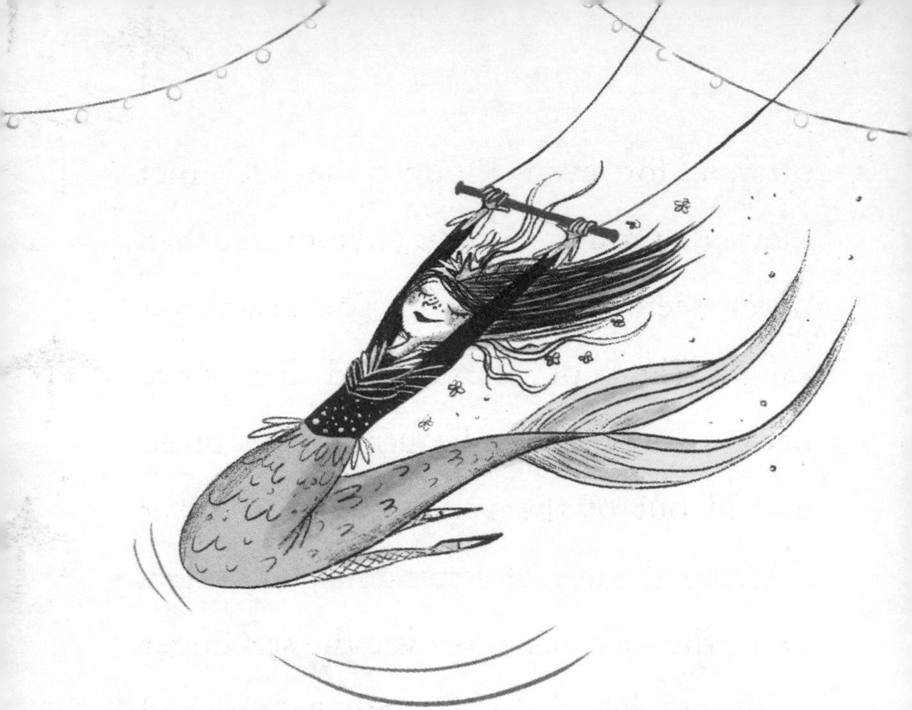

turquoise. It was incredibly crowded, but Isabella could just make out a pool of shimmering water in the centre. Then the air seemed to sizzle, as above them a woman swung into the light on a trapeze. She was dressed as a mermaid and had a voice as lovely as ocean waves.

"So this is the sea-singer," Isabella

uttered, for even though she had met Harper's mother, Aurelia, before, she had never seen her perform. The sea-singer caught sight of Harper and her voice became even more beautiful. She dived in and out of the water, her song never faltering, the crowd gasping in amazement. Once the spectacle was over, the sea-singer embraced her daughter. Isabella watched the cheering crowds and again found herself wishing that she was part of this glorious and strange circus.

A huge shadow fell across the tent, Quite suddenly, Aurelia let go of Harper and seemed to scurry away in fear, as a large man with a bristly red beard barged his way forwards. Isabella and Harper both took a step backwards. They had never seen the man before but they could guess who he was: Othello Grande, the ringmaster. With a quick glance at her mother, Harper pulled Isabella away, and they set off to explore more tents. But neither of them was able to shake away the unsettling memory of the man with the red beard.

Ferdie came careering towards them, proudly brandishing his pencil. Harper clasped his hands. "Are you going to be a world-famous poet?" she asked.

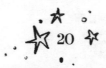

Ferdie shook his head, but his eyes were bright as newborn stars. "No," he cried triumphantly, "I'll be a struggling playwright." Here his voice trailed off as he imagined the quiet glory of living in the attic of the Tall Apartment Block, with only his serious scarf to keep him warm as he typed away on a rickety typewriter.

"What a wonderful life it will be," he sighed.

"Hey," piped up a happy voice, interrupting Ferdie's daydream. It was Liesel and her friend Rat, who were merrily munching on toffee apples. "Rat's doing a show with his dazzling Rat Dancers in five minutes," yelped Liesel excitedly, beckoning them over the bridge. "We have to see it!"

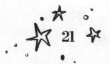

Isabella nodded dreamily and the little group turned to follow Liesel into a striped tent. Then Harper caught sight of Nate and Smoke on the other side of the cloud. The sleek silvery wolf, who was usually a creature of superior grace, seemed strangely wild-eyed. "Is everything OK?" she asked, wandering over to them.

Nate nodded and ran his hands over the wolf, soothing her back to calm her. "We found a bridge that didn't quite feel the same as the others. It seemed to go down instead of over, and it seemed as old and delicate as cobwebs."

Harper frowned. She had never come across anything like that in the circus. "Where was it?" she asked. Nate pointed into the distance, but Harper couldn't see anything other than bobbing, colourful tents.

"Come on! The show's about to start,"

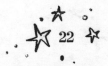

squeaked Liesel, popping her head out of the striped tent. Nate grinned and let Harper lead him into the tent, but all through the performance he couldn't help wondering where the strange cobwebby bridge might lead to...

Chapter Three
THE WILD CONDUCTOR'S WISH

By the time the children had hugged their friends at the circus goodbye and followed Nate back to the Tall Apartment Block, twilight was falling. City lights flickered like far-off stars, and the night felt still and magical. As everyone hurried to the rooftop, Harper opened her Scarlet

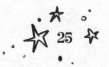

Umbrella and drifted up ahead of them, picking Midnight up along the way. She had a very important announcement to make.

Beneath the gathering dusk, Harper spun the Scarlet Umbrella upside down and stood inside it, hovering just high enough to see everyone's faces.

"As you all know," she began, "I promised to help the Wild Conductor win back his place in the Circus of Dreams by putting on an amazing show." Everyone's eyes twinkled. "And as the Circus is here, I think we should put on the show tonight."

At this, the crowd looked confused. Peter, a world-famous writer who was Ferdie and Liesel's father, stepped forward.

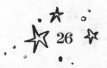

"That's a wonderful idea, little Harp," he said fondly, "but we haven't rehearsed."

Madame Flora, the ballet teacher from the third floor, curtsied anxiously. "But Harper is right," she breathed, "we need to catch the circus before the wind changes and sweeps it away."

Isabella approached, bringing her entire family with her, each of them holding up a drum. "We will help however we can," they cried, accidentally clashing a cymbal and startling many of the cats.

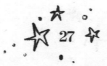

Then a voice that crackled with the splendour of age spoke up: "Harper, why don't you tell them your plan?" It was Elsie Caraham, the oldest resident of the Tall Apartment Block. Her green cloak billowed in the evening breeze, making her look quite powerful.

"The Wild Conductor has been rehearsing for months," Harper said, "practising songs on the cloudian while I listened from the rooftop." The crowd began to whisper with excitement. "At the stroke of twelve tonight he'll perform and you will be the audience."

At once, everyone set off to fetch blankets and deckchairs, so they could watch the concert from the roof. Madame Flora sashayed forward on rose-pink points. "What is the cloudian?" she asked.

"You'll see." Harper giggled and then she quickly added, "Oh, and please all bring your umbrellas!"

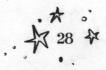

As midnight approached, everybody sat in perfect stillness, umbrellas open above their heads, handles clutched proudly to their hearts. Harper, Ferdie, Liesel and Nate stood slightly to one side with Elsie Caraham.

Liesel gave a long, impatient sigh. She found all this waiting around incredibly boring. "Why does the Wild Conductor want to rejoin the circus anyway?" she pondered.

"Because it's the most amazing place in the entire world?" suggested Nate, yet they all knew there was more to it than that.

"Maybe it's to do with power," said Ferdie doubtfully, for that didn't seem right either.

"It might be to do with family," Harper suggested.

"Or love," added Elsie Caraham knowingly.

Liesel burst out laughing. "He's far too grumpy to fall in love," she declared.

"Well, perhaps he's simply heartbroken," Elsie continued.

The children stared at each other in bewilderment. They'd never really thought of that.

At that moment, clocks all over the City of Clouds began to chime midnight. Harper held her breath – it was time for the show to begin!

At the twelfth stroke came a soft clinking of silver, like the spinning chain of a bike. Everyone turned to follow the sound and froze in astonishment as the Wild Conductor came gently peddling across the sky on a bicycle attached to a shimmering cloud. The bicycle was black as thunder and the cloud was the colour of starlight, and they were bound together with stems of edentwine. It was a most magnificent sight.

"So this is the cloudian," murmured Madame Flora, and Harper gave a happy nod. When the Wild Conductor cycled faster, the twine hugged the cloud and a shower of musical raindrops tumbled down over the roof. And what a song it was – a song all the way from the Night Forest that could tame the fiercest of hearts. The

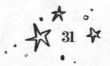

residents leaped up off their blankets and out of their deckchairs, their hearts alight with hope.

Liesel popped open her pink-and-grey umbrella, which had little ears like a mouse, and started to dance across the roof. As she twirled high on her toes there came a soft whooshing like the sound of a shooting star and, to her utter delight, Liesel found she was dancing on air.

Chapter Four
A FLOCK OF FLYING UMBRELLAS

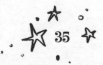

Ferdie gave a wondrous shout as his sister drifted up towards the sparkling sky. Until that moment it had only ever been Harper's enchanted Scarlet Umbrella that had been able to fly. But as the spell of the cloudian's song rained down, all the umbrellas began jostling and hovering and rising into the air. Many of the residents had never flown before and they gasped to see the City of Clouds spread out below them. From up high its flickering lights made it dazzle like a city of fireflies.

Then, without any warning, Ferdie's green umbrella barged into Nate, shoving him roughly sideways and making both boys wobble. There was a yell from Elsie Caraham as Great Aunt Sassy's purple umbrella knocked off her emerald cape, and a squeal from Isabella as her orange umbrella went spinning into Madame Flora, sending her whirling across the sky, a single silken point shoe falling to the roof.

"The umbrellas are out of control!" cried Nate, struggling to regain his balance.

Quicker than lightning, Harper spun the Scarlet Umbrella upside down and dived into it like a little red boat. Midnight darted off her shoulder and into the umbrella's folds, hooking his claw around a small golden harp and tugging it on to Harper's lap. Harper lifted it high and at once began to play. The moment the music of the harp met with the music of the cloudian, everything calmed, as if an invisible wave of peace had swept through the sky. One by one the umbrellas stopped crashing into each other and became a softly floating flock once more.

The Wild Conductor adjusted his terribly tall top hat and bowed his head to Harper. This had not been part of the plan.

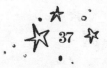

He alone had hoped to tame the fierce heart of Othello Grande, as the rules for entering the Circus of Dreams were very strict. He had to:

Summon them with a talent. Charm them with a skill. Or put on a performance that would make their hearts stand still.

And yet, as he watched the child in the Scarlet Umbrella with the rare musical gift, the Wild Conductor realized that her talent only added to the wonder of the show, and he peddled on merrily, sending droplets of musical rain all the way to the red-and-gold tent.

There was a swirling of dark cloud and the residents of the Tall Apartment Block clutched their umbrellas closer.

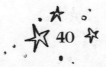

"I think the circus is coming!" whispered Liesel, who could hardly contain her excitement.

Nate reached out a hand and felt the air, giving a swift nod. Thunder cracked the sky, but Harper and the Wild Conductor held their nerve, keeping the music flowing. Black clouds parted and a flight of stormy birds emerged, each of them towing a far-off tent. They dived amongst the umbrellas, filling the night with feathers and drawing the magnificent circus closer, until it lingered in the air just above everyone's heads.

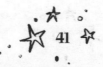

Harper, Ferdie and Liesel all peered upwards, trying to spot their friends the storm-stirrers. But instead they found themselves staring into the beady eyes of a man with a huge red beard and a cruel heart.

Nate, who could hear the beating

of mighty wings, drifted a little nearer to Harper. "What's happening?" he asked.

"Othello Grande is here," she breathed. "I think we've done it! I think the Wild Conductor has won back his place in the Cir—"

But at that moment Liesel screamed and Ferdie gave a panicked yell. Harper hardly had time to gasp before a huge white-winged eagle swooped towards her, seizing the Scarlet Umbrella's handle in its claws.

Nate felt the nearness of the great bird and knew he had to help Harper. Bravely, he cast his own umbrella aside and seized the spike of the Scarlet Umbrella in his hands. As the mighty bird pulled both children higher into the air, Nate managed to wedge his foot into the branches of a rooftop tree, so they were caught in a sky-high tug of war.

The Wild Conductor stared up in confusion as Othello's bird tried to steal Harper. "Othello, what are you doing?" he cried. "Leave the child alone! If the cloudian's song has tamed your heart, you must let me back into the circus. If not, then you must leave."

Othello gave a sickly chuckle. "And leave I will," he hissed, "but not without the girl who plays the harp."

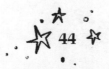

And with that, Othello snapped his pudgy fingers and the great bird's wings beat the air, yanking the Scarlet Umbrella out of Nate's hand and dragging Harper and Midnight into the folds of the red-and-gold tent.

"Somebody save them!" bellowed Great Aunt Sassy.

Ferdie and Liesel, who were used to flying by umbrella, raced across the sky, sending the other residents tumbling out the way. Liesel dived towards Nate, who was slipping through starlight. She spun her mouse-eared umbrella upside down, balanced upon its handle on one foot, and caught Nate like a dancer. Ferdie tried to follow the great bird, but a fierce whirlwind of cloud blotted out the moon and he found himself in darkness.

Then the air cleared and so did the strange white mist. A heartbeat of rain fell from the sky, washing away the magic. Everyone gazed around in shock, for the Circus of Dreams was nowhere to be seen. It had stolen Harper and Midnight and vanished into thin air.

Chapter Five
A BRILLIANT PLAN

"Someone must save my darling Harper!" Great Aunt Sassy wailed.

The Wild Conductor turned quite pale, his heart filling with despair, his feet slowing on the peddles. "I will go after the circus," he said, knowing that this was all his fault. All around him umbrellas wobbled unsteadily back to the rooftop and a nervous mumbling swept through the crowd.

"We'll come with you," called Nate.

The Wild Conductor frowned darkly. "There isn't room on the cloudian," he said sadly.

But Ferdie was already attaching his green umbrella to the black bicycle with a strand of Edentwine, a gleam in his eye. "If you peddle really fast, our umbrellas will fly on the cloudian's song."

The Wild Conductor gave a weak nod. "Hurry then," he said. "We must leave at once."

Liesel pushed her filthy hair out of her eyes and helped Nate on to the back of the bike, while Ferdie quickly set to work attaching his sister's umbrella to the black bicycle. Nate gave a low whistle and Smoke came racing through midnight clouds with Nate's green umbrella clasped tightly in her powerful jaws. With a wonderful bound, she landed on Nate's lap, making the black bicycle spin dangerously.

A small cheer arose from the residents, and even Great Aunt Sassy managed a small grin. Then the black bicycle with a man in a sweeping satin coat and a boy with a wolf began to sail across the sky, towing two brightly coloured umbrellas behind.

Madame Flora danced gracefully forwards and plucked a huge storm bloom, tossing it up so that Ferdie caught it. "For

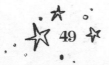

luck," she smiled, blowing them each a kiss.

Liesel looked at the flower and gave a brave laugh. "We don't need luck – we know the circus better than anyone." But she gripped her umbrella tightly all the same as they journeyed through the night.

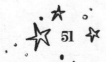

For a long while no one in the little group spoke, the sadness of the situation weighing on each of them. But gradually the beauty of the night calmed their beating hearts and they began to enjoy the journey. Sometimes they caught a glimpse of lightning on the horizon or passed a floating eagle feather, so they knew they were on the right track. The Wild Conductor peddled like his life depended on it, never taking his eyes from the far-off storm.

Liesel, who was used to travelling at this height, watched the Wild Conductor closely. She had known him a long time, but she realized now that she didn't really know that much about him. "Ferdie!" she hissed.

Ferdie was dreaming up a poem about the beauty of dawn, and he stared in surprise. "What?"

"We have to find out exactly why the Wild Conductor wants to get back into the circus," said Liesel. "We need to know why he and Othello hate each other."

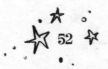

Ferdie straightened up and leaned forwards until he was flying level with the pale-faced man. "You need to tell us why the Circus of Dreams is so important to you," he said. The Wild Conductor scowled, but Ferdie insisted. "Please, it might help us rescue Harper."

For a moment there was silence, then the tall man answered. "Very well."

And so, as they soared through feather-fern cloud and streaks of first sunshine, the Wild Conductor began to tell his tale.

"Once, many years ago, when I was still a young man," he began, "I lived happily in the Circus of Dreams. Othello Grande was my friend. He was a young man too and had just taken over the circus from his parents. He was sorry to give up his act to run the show, but happy to welcome me in his place."

Liesel, who adored stories but had very little patience, shouted out, "So what went wrong?"

The Wild Conductor smiled sadly. "There was a girl in the circus called Star."

"Ah," whispered Ferdie with a triumphant grin, "so it was love."

The Wild Conductor ignored Ferdie and went on. "She was called the Fire Star, because whenever she heard music she began to shine like a star. She needed no tightrope – no strings or wings – she simply glowed and rose into the air. A girl with a heart made of fire. When Star jumped, it truly looked like she was a firework."

The Wild Conductor paused here and

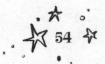

Nate, who was very close, noticed how the tall man's eyes had become misted with the memory.

"When I played the songs I'd written, Star shone brighter than ever," said the Wild Conductor fondly. "Othello soon became jealous. Then one day, a spark from Star's glowing heart landed in Othello's beard and it singed his red beard black. The audience roared with laughter, so he flew into a hateful rage and banished Star from the circus."

"What a spiteful man!" exclaimed Liesel, who loved the idea of a girl with a heart of fire.

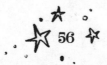

"I couldn't let Star get turned out of the circus all alone, so I pleaded with Othello to let her stay and kick me out instead. I thought with time I could charm the circus and be part of it once again."

The little group were silent as they realized just how brave the Wild Conductor had been. "So all this time you've been trying to get back to the circus to find Star?" asked Nate.

The Wild Conductor hung his head. "It's taken a great many more years than I'd hoped," he said flatly.

"Are you sure that Star is still in the circus?" asked Liesel, trying to remember if she'd ever seen her act.

"Yes," said the Wild Conductor simply.

Ferdie tightened his serious scarf. "If there's one thing I know for certain," he announced, "it's that Othello Grande needs to be stopped."

Everyone nodded and, as they flew on, the three children huddled closely at the back of the bike thinking up a brilliant plan.

"The first thing we need to do," Nate whispered, "is send Harper a signal so she knows we are coming."

With a poetic flourish Ferdie produced the storm bloom. "Let's send her this flower – they only grow in the City of Clouds." He grinned and then gave a serious frown. "I'm just not sure how we get it to her."

Liesel gave her knotted hair a wild shake, awakening the little pink dove that was comfortable nesting in her tangles. "Storm can fly much faster than us. If she could catch up with the circus, she could deliver the storm bloom to Harper."

Nate nodded brightly and Ferdie reached for the pencil he kept tucked behind his ear and began scribbling a note upon the flower's dusky petals. "Let's tell Harper to find out all she can about the Fire Star," he added in a hushed voice.

The others agreed, then Liesel let the little dove clasp the flower's stem in her sharp beak, and sent her arcing into the air like an arrow of feathers aimed straight for the heart of the circus.

Chapter Six
INSIDE THE CIRCUS

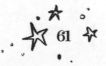

On the other side of sunrise, as morning arrived, Harper scrambled to her feet. She was in complete darkness, caught up in a chaos of scarlet fabric and cat fur. Midnight purred around her ankles, telling her they were somewhere familiar. And as Harper reached out and ran her hands over thick velvet curtains, she realized she was inside the lightning-leader's tent.

"But where is the lightning-leader?" Harper whispered, feeling both joy to be back in the circus and fear that she might never be able to leave.

At that moment the velvet curtain began to softly rustle and she froze. Then her parents' strong arms were embracing her. "Mum! Dad!" Harper cried, wilting with relief.

Aurelia's sea-grey eyes were overflowing with tears. "Harper," she smiled, "thank goodness you're safe."

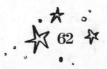

Hugo swept Harper into a biscuit-scented hug. "You have to pretend you don't know us," he said, his face suddenly serious. Harper gulped.

Aurelia clasped her hand. "If Othello finds out you're the girl who escaped the circus, he will never let you out of his sight."

Harper gave them the best grin she could summon. "It shouldn't be too difficult," she beamed. For even though Harper's parents were clearly worried about her, she felt a secret surge of glee at finally being allowed to perform with the circus.

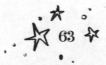

Heavy footsteps shook the cloud beneath them, and the lightning-leader appeared and ushered Hugo and Aurelia away. Then she stood beside Harper, her aura crackling with blue light, and whispered, "Just try not to anger Othello." Harper barely had time to nod and scoop Midnight up before a man with an enormous red beard squeezed into the tent.

"Welcome to my circus of wonders and wishes," came the snake-like voice. Harper said nothing, but she clutched Midnight closely. "You appear to have a most marvellous musical gift," Othello went on. "How would you like to be part of my magical circus?"

Harper forced a smile. "I would like it very much," she murmured.

"Very good," said Othello snidely. "We will write to your family and tell them that from now on you will live here among the clouds."

Harper said nothing, thinking how sad it must be for performers who desperately wanted to go home.

Othello's thick brow furrowed and his enormous beard loomed over Harper. "And tell me," he said in a low voice, "what do you know of the Wild Conductor?"

"Nothing much, really," she mumbled. "He's a friend of my Great Aunt Sassy."

Othello scowled. "You will not mention his name ever again!"

Midnight gave a fierce meow and, to Harper's horror, he broke out of her arms and tried to bite the big man on the leg, which made Harper want to laugh.

"We don't allow pets in the circus!" Othello boomed, picking Midnight up by the scruff off the neck and moving towards the entrance of the tent.

Harper's eyes opened wide with dismay. "But he has to stay with me," she pleaded. "He's my everything, my best friend, my ... my..." But her voice trailed off.

"My dearest Othello," said the lightning-leader smoothly, "this is no pet. This cat is part of the child's act."

Othello glared at Midnight with an expression that reminded Harper of a small, angry pig. Quickly, Harper fished her piccolo flute out of her pocket and threw it into the air. Midnight caught it in his teeth and at once began to play, filling the tent with a merry little ditty that miraculously made Othello chuckle.

He put the cat down and folded his arms across his chest. "Very well," he said. "But the cat must work to earn his keep."

Harper buried her face in Midnight's dark fur.

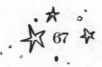

"You can start rehearsals today," Othello went on. "Wherever the circus next stops, you and your cat must perform." Then he swung around, his frame filling up most of the tent, and squeezed back out into the daylight.

"Well done," smiled the lightning-leader, stroking Harper's dark hair from her brow and guiding her out of the other end of the tent. To Harper's delight she found a wild crew of ragtag children waiting for her: the storm-stirrers.

"Come with us," beamed Skylar, the chief storm-stirrer. "We'll help you put on a show that will knock Othello's socks off."

Harper had never felt so grateful. How would she ever have managed in this vast and mysterious circus without her friends? She ran with the others to the Heavens of the Circus, a landscape of huge umbrella tops that looked like silken moons. She was ready to meet the children's orchestra and put on a spectacular act! If she could just fool Othello into thinking she was happy in the Circus of Dreams, he would never suspect she was planning to escape.

Chapter Seven
THE STORM BLOOM

Harper's day passed in a dazzle of tightropes and trapezes and tremendous tricks. As the first distant stars began to awaken, it was time for one final rehearsal.

Some of the storm-stirrers gathered around, pretending to be the audience, whilst the rest rushed to their positions.

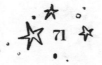

Harper leaped lightly into the Scarlet Umbrella and whispered, "Ready, boy?"

Midnight gave a happy meow and, as they rose into the air, Harper set her little cat down on the umbrella's scarlet edge. He prowled around it on dainty paws, playing the piccolo flute with his teeth and tail. He looked quite wonderful.

Harper climbed up, balancing on her tiptoes on the top of the upside-down umbrella's silver handle. She raised her golden harp into the air, her fingers dancing across its strings as delicately as dove wings, filling the sky with a harmony of hope: a tune of swirling clouds and long-lost dreams that made the storm-stirrers gasp.

As Harper played, the Scarlet Umbrella began to spin round and round dizzyingly fast, but Harper

looked only at Midnight and ignored the whirling world and excited cheers of her friends. Then a storm-stirrer called Sunbeam swung past her on a trapeze and threw a large bassoon over her shoulder. Harper caught it with a single hand, tooted on it loudly, and flung the bassoon high for Sunbeam to catch it as she swung back the other way.

Next, Liesel's friend Rat cartwheeled past on a tightrope, hurling Harper a set of cymbals that she clashed and bashed and threw behind her for Rat to grab with his feet. Slowly, more storm-stirrers came zooming past on the backs of great birds, or simply free-diving, or running along invisible wires, throwing

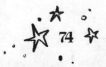

Harper instruments in a musical madness of juggling and twirling. The umbrella sped up with the song until Harper and Midnight became a blur of scarlet silk with the flash of a white-tipped tail.

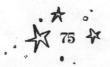

Storm-stirrers leaped to their feet applauding, and Harper felt a rush of wonderment. *So this is what it's like to be a performer.* She laughed, understanding suddenly why people gave their whole lives to it, for the joy of the wild circus was like nothing she had ever known. For a single heartbeat Harper wondered if perhaps there was a way she could stay here and be happy. But then she remembered her parents' courage: how they risked everything to smuggle her out of the circus, away from the temper of Othello Grande.

The song ended and Harper half toppled on to the indigo balloon. She was tired and dizzy, but her eyes were dancing with happiness. The storm-stirrers crowded close, embracing Harper in a warm hug. "That was brilliant!" beamed Skylar.

Harper felt her cheeks begin to glow. "Thank you," she mumbled, settling herself next to Rat and gathering up Midnight. She gazed across the evening sky and realized that the circus must have left the City of Clouds long ago, for the sky was a dazzle of stars, each of them bright and wondrous. All of a sudden she felt a jab of loneliness. Though the circus was extraordinary and enchanting and held mysteries as deep as the sea, it was not the Tall Apartment Block.

Harper quietly excused herself from the rehearsal and slipped away, wandering to the edge of the Heavens of the Circus. She scanned the sweeping horizon for something familiar but found nothing. "Oh, Midnight," she whispered, feeling a heaviness settle on her as swift and deep as snow.

Something flickered in the distance and Harper's heart gave the tiniest leap. A bird the same colour as blossom was dipping and diving towards her. In its beak it held a dusky grey flower that only blooms in the rain. Harper gasped as the little bird looped the air above her, dropping the flower into her hands, and then spun into the sky, swooping away. She clutched the flower to her chest and followed the bird with her eyes.

Far, far away, on the other side of the

sunset, a tiny black shape was peddling into the wind. Peddling like his life depended on it. Peddling on an instrument sewn from silver-lined cloud.

"Midnight," Harper breathed, "I think the Wild Conductor is coming to save us!"

At that moment, the circus gave a strange jolt and a furious wind began to howl all around it. Harper stepped back from the edge, hiding the storm bloom in her pocket.

In a burst of grace and feathers, Skylar appeared beside her. "The circus has stopped for the night," she explained. "We need to go and stir up the white mist, so tomorrow we can arrive at a nearby town in secret."

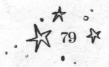

Harper nodded and gave a small smile. There was a whirring of fast feet as the rest of storm-stirrers sprang on to the backs of great birds and swooped away.

Chapter Eight
THE OTHER BRIDGE

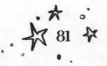

A little way off from the circus, on a black bicycle softly winding its way through the night, the Wild Conductor sighed. No one was more relieved that the circus had stopped than him. He had been peddling hard all day and was quite exhausted. He brought the cloudian and its trail of bright umbrellas in to land. But his legs were so shaky with tiredness that, as he tried to climb off the black bicycle, he fell flat on his face instead. Liesel had to smother a giggle whilst Ferdie tightened his serious scarf and performed a poem:

"Tall man on the bike who flew so high,
Through the dark and starry sky,
Do not despair, do not lose heart,
Just have a bite of treacle tart."

And, as if by magic, Ferdie held out a squashed bit of pie crust that had been in his pocket for many months. The Wild Conductor managed a weary smile.

The little bunch gazed around at their

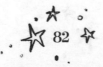

surroundings and saw they were in the middle of rolling fields. In the distance shone the gentle lights of a sleepy village. Tomorrow the village would awaken to the wonderful sight of a floating circus. But tonight they slept on, unaware of the magic unfolding above them.

The Wild Conductor bid each of the children goodnight and curled up like a very big, ungainly cat and started snoring.

Nate took pity on the tall man's fragile heart and carefully arranged the three umbrellas over him like a toadstool-shaped tent. Then he turned to his two friends. "Let's get some supper," he said with a stretch. "Then we'll see if there's another way into the circus."

Liesel gave a bright-eyed blink. "What do you mean?"

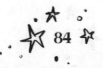

Nate shrugged and gave Smoke a pat. "I'm not exactly sure, but last time I was there Smoke found a bridge that was different to all the others. It felt as if it were made from cobwebs and it seemed to dip down instead of up and over."

Liesel's eyes grew wide. "Where do you think it leads?" she pondered.

"Not sure," answered Nate, "but if Star really is still in the circus, then maybe there's more to the place then we can see."

Ferdie closed his eyes, imagining what Nate might mean. "Like other tents that are hidden?" he asked. Nate nodded.

Liesel's toes twitched with excitement. "If I was trying to hide a tent, I'd pitch it beneath the circus, in the middle of all the white mist – that way no one would notice it." And before anyone could stop her she leaped aboard the cloudian, wobbling wildly as she tried to balance its weight. "Come on, let's fly beneath the circus and see what's going on."

All at once, all thoughts of food were forgotten, because if there is ever choice between supper or an adventure aboard a flying bike, peddled by a mouse-loving girl, adventure will always win. Besides, Ferdie's pockets turned out to be stuffed with other squashed-but-edible things, that didn't taste too awful. He, Nate and Smoke crowded on to the back of the bike and, as a lullaby of sweetly pattering rain splashed upon the bright umbrella, the cloudian rose splendidly into the air.

The Wild Conductor slept on, hardly hearing the lullaby or even wondering what the pleasant sound might be. For his dreams were filled with only one person:

a girl with a heart of fire, who shone as bright as a star.

In his dream he wandered through a world of swirling white, a world that felt empty of colour and magic. It was a dream he often had, both brilliant and terrifying at once – brilliant because he got to see the face of his true love once again, but terrifying because she was no longer shining. In desperation the Wild Conductor played every song he knew, but alas his music could never touch Star and she turned sadly away, a trail of ash spilling behind her where once there were sparks.

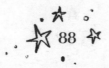

Chapter Nine
THE ABANDONED TENT

High above the clump of bright umbrellas, Harper was wandering through the circus. All around its edges a whirlwind raged, but inside Harper felt safe. A night breeze tugged at the canvas tents and blew Harper's dark hair across her face, and she tripped over a tent wire and went crashing into someone. As Harper swiped her hair out of her sea-grey eyes, she saw to her horror that she'd crashed into Othello Grande.

"Where are you off to in such a hurry?" came the snide voice as he leered over Harper, his frame darkening the moon.

"I..." began Harper breathlessly. She stared bravely into his small, beady eyes. "I was just looking for my little cat," she said brightly, spotting Midnight somewhere up ahead of her.

Othello looked at her slyly. "Well, let's hope you find him before I do," he half spat. "I can't have any pets running amok in my circus."

Harper nodded calmly and scurried away. She gazed around wildly for Midnight.

But it seemed the tale she'd told Othello had come true, for the mysterious black cat was nowhere to be seen.

Harper darted and dashed over bridge after bridge calling for her cat, but Midnight did not appear. A whirl of worry whipped about her heart. Where could he have got to? Then Harper's foot slipped and she found herself sinking into a cloud all the way up to her knees. In a panic she reached out to grab the handles of the bridge she was on, but they came apart in her hands like cobwebs. Whatever she was standing on was some sort of bridge that led below the circus. A bridge spun from spidersilk. A bridge you would never be able to find if you were looking for it.

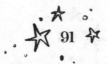

Harper stopped still. *Of course!* she thought. *This is the bridge Nate found.* And she was right. Nate was a boy who never *looked* for anything; he felt his way through the world. It was no wonder he had discovered a secret pathway.

A playful meow echoed up from somewhere far below, and Harper realized with a soft sense of dread that Midnight must have crossed the downwards bridge. She took a breath and began to edge slowly away from the colourful world of the circus and into swaths of swirling mist.

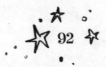

At once Harper felt the air go cold, as if it was made of sea-fog or floating droplets of rain. She shivered and crept forwards, noticing that the bridge was hardly a bridge at all but more of slanting stairway that lead steeply down. With every step the cloud thickened. Harper was used to clouds – she lived in a city named after them. But this cloud was different. It was both starless and silent and glowed an eerie shade of grey.

Then Harper saw something that stole the very air from her lungs. In front of her, rising out of the shadows like the spire of a haunted tower, was a tent as ghostly and strange as a graveyard. As she stared at it, Harper saw a little black cat with a white-tipped tail slip neatly under the closed doorway and vanish inside. "No, Midnight," she groaned, but it was too late – Midnight had already entered the tent.

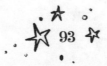

Bravely, Harper opened her Scarlet Umbrella and tried to zoom down to the tent's towering entrance. But, to her amazement, the umbrella floundered and twirled on the spot, as if flying was a great effort. Harper clasped the handle tightly and commanded it to move. With great difficulty the umbrella floated downwards, as if it were drifting through a dream – the sort of dream a wolf might have in winter. For, as Harper looked down, she saw that everything was bleak white, pale grey or swirling hopeless black.

She found the doorway of the abandoned tent padlocked shut, but with a prod from the umbrella the lock came away in a pile of scattered rust. Harper steeled herself and

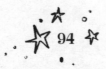

ducked inside. It was dark and cobwebby, but absolutely enormous – by far the biggest tent in the circus. Harper shuffled forwards, her feet kicking up something soft and fluttery, like the ash of burned silk.

What happened here? Harper wondered, gazing around with a sense of fearful wonder. She caught sight of Midnight in the farthest corner of the tent, curled up happily on top of a beautiful old dressing table. Harper smiled with relief and crossed the huge tent, noticing that it was full of props and circus fliers, as if a show had come to a sudden halt halfway through – or time had simply stopped.

Something on the ashen floor caught her eye. It was a poster that had been badly burned. The only word Harper could read on it was STAR in shimmering gold. "Perhaps there was some sort of fire here," Harper said, scooping Midnight up and giving him a kiss. He held a scroll of singed paper in his jaws. Harper prised it out and discovered that it was sheet music. The paper itself was very old and frail, and in the dark of the abandoned tent she couldn't read the tune, but she rolled it up and slipped it into her pocket all the same.

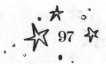

The strange mystery of the place was beginning to fascinate Harper, and she explored a little further, stumbling over a huge wooden trunk. The lid was heavy but, with a sharp tug, it lifted. A cloud of dusk-coloured moths filled the air, tickling Midnight's nose and making Harper laugh. But as the moths cleared she felt her mouth fall open, for folded carefully at the bottom of the trunk was the most glorious costume she had ever set eyes on. Harper couldn't help but touch it, lifting it delicately out of the trunk so she could admire its dazzling beauty. It was a cross between a ballerina's tutu and a firework, embroidered with flame-coloured stars, so that even in the half darkness it seemed to move like fire.

"Who does this belong too?" Harper gasped, running her fingers over each diamond-cut star. Midnight suddenly arched his back and gave a hissing meow.

Harper clutched the costume and froze. Ever so softly came the sound of footsteps. There was someone else in the abandoned tent.

Almost without thinking, Harper grabbed Midnight and ran. As she shot out of the entrance she popped the Scarlet Umbrella open and willed it to fly. It rose uncertainly, but not fast enough. Harper felt the danger before she saw it – the gleam of bright eyes watching her. She glanced down to see a lone figure stood in the doorway of the tent. The figure was draped in robes of black and seemed to shimmer like smoke. Her hair was the same brilliant red as the Scarlet Umbrella, and it fell around her face like the flattened

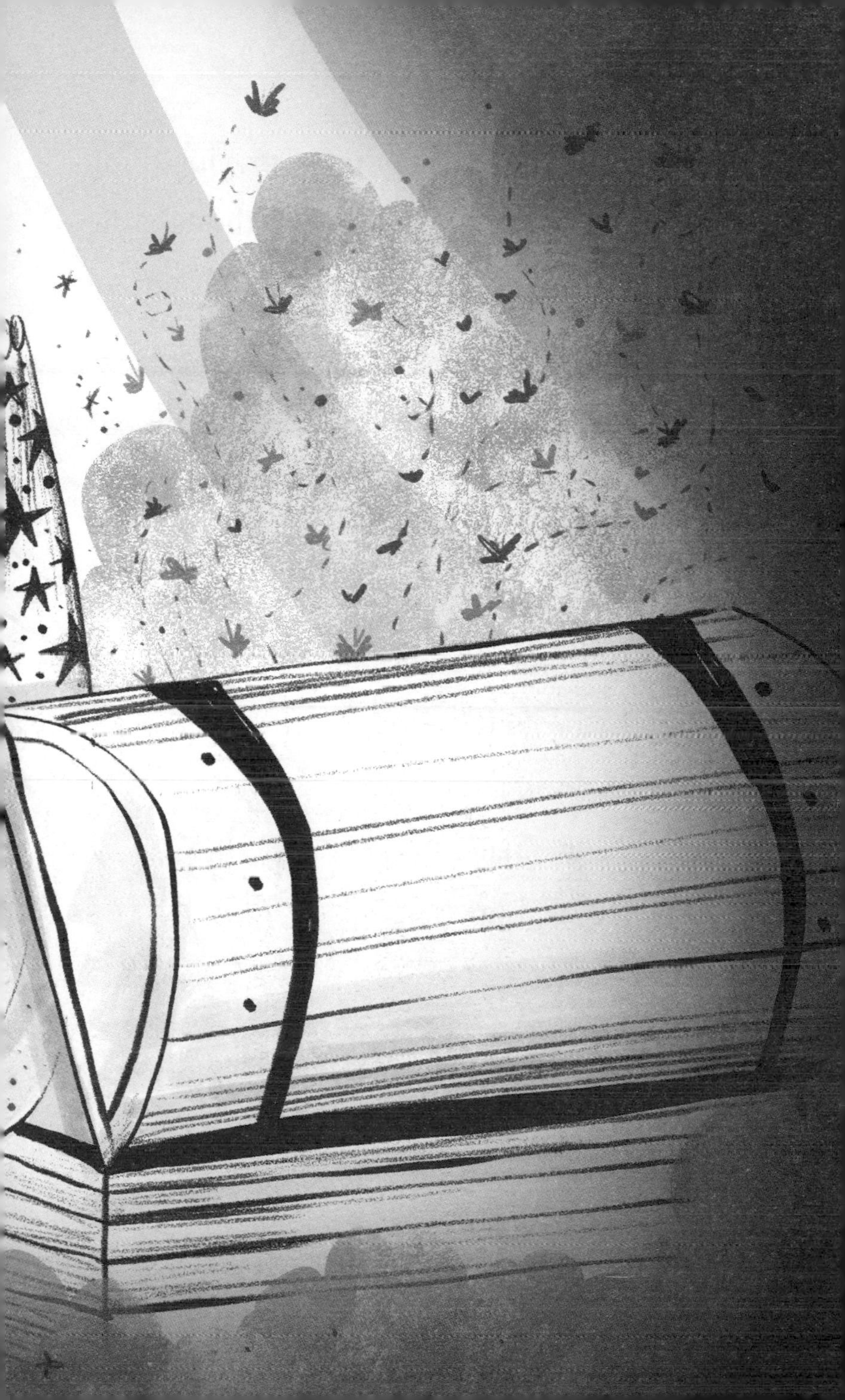

points of a star. But the most striking thing about her was her eyes. For though she had an ice-queen beauty, her eyes glowed like embers. She was not like anyone else in the circus. She was not like anyone else in the world. A woman trapped in a dream of winter, with a heart as fierce as fire.

She began to stalk towards the drifting umbrella. Harper tried to be brave, tried to look into the woman's ember eyes, but she found herself shaking. The woman reached out a hand

towards Harper's foot as if to pluck her from the air.

Then a note of music cut through the cloud, startling them both. It was soft and bright and magical. A song of dark forests and moonlight wings. A song played on an instrument sewn from silver-lined cloud.

"The cloudian!" Harper gasped suddenly, realizing that her friends must be near. At once the Scarlet Umbrella jolted upwards, away from the woman with ember eyes and towards the colourful world of the circus.

As quickly as she could, Harper wrestled herself, the umbrella and Midnight through the little gap in the cloud. She peered behind her, searching for a glimpse of the black bicycle, but only saw the ember-eyed woman gazing at her in bewilderment – no longer shimmering like smoke but ever so softly glowing. Then white mist clouded Harper's view and the land beneath the circus vanished from sight.

She stumbled to her feet. Somewhere on the other side of the storm were her friends – she had to find them.

Chapter Ten
THE LAND BELOW

Deep in the land below the circus, the cloudian was whirling around in whiteness.

"I can't see anything," Liesel roared, trying desperately to pedal.

"Let Nate steer," Ferdie urged, hoping his friend would be able to find his bearings. But finding your way in the air is different to finding your way on the ground. Without a single landmark or sound to guide him, Nate was as lost as the others. It was Smoke who howled and snarled and growled the way forwards, somehow managing to direct them into a patch of stillness.

The children at once felt the world grow colder, and even though Nate was peddling as fast as he could, he found his feet would only move in slow-motion. Liesel shivered. Even she was a little unnerved by the quiet of this place. The song of the cloudian slowed until it sounded haunting and strange. "Where are we?" asked Ferdie.

"We're somewhere near the cobweb

bridge," Nate answered, "somewhere under the circus."

And that's when they caught sight of a glimpse of scarlet – a girl with an enchanted umbrella disappearing upwards. "Harper," Liesel screamed, but Harper didn't seem to be able to hear her, as if sound itself moved at a slower speed.

All the three friends could do was watch as their friend disappeared away from them. Then Ferdie saw the strange glittering figure who stood below them. "There's a woman in the clouds who is ... sparkling," Ferdie whispered to Nate.

A single spark fell from the woman's heart, turning the air gold. Liesel watched her intently. It seemed as if with every note of music from the cloudian the figure shone a little brighter. But the song was slowing down, becoming more and more eerie, until every drop of sound seemed to vanish into the swirling greyness of the world.

Ferdie, Liesel and Nate hardly had time to think before the cloudian started toppling with a dreamlike slowness, slipping through the air, its last drops of magic peeling away. The children went into a state of panic. You see, the cloudian was an important part of the rescue plan. If it couldn't fly, then they wouldn't be able to save Harper.

"We have to get out of here," yelled Nate, but no amount of steering or cycling would do it, and the bike continued to fall.

"If we can't go up then we'll have to go down," yelled Liesel.

Nate at once understood what she meant and fastened a strand of edentwine to Smoke's collar. "Go, girl," he whispered, and with a snapping of wild jaws and a breathtaking bound, the wolf leaped through the grey skies, her claws seeming to slice through the mist.

The woman with ember eyes watched with astonishment as the weight of the wolf pulled the cloudian down and the children shot past her, soaring towards open fields and a man snoring beneath a mushroom-shaped tent. As the cloud split open the woman gave a rare but radiant smile, then reached out, not to stop the

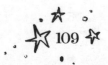

cloudian, but to try and come with them, only the cloud whirled back around her, holding her for ever in the dark dream of winter.

"Peddle!" bellowed Nate, and they did, all three of them, sending notes of musical rain hurtling down to the ground in a shower of spiky sound. The Wild

Conductor awoke and leaped to his feet, just in time to catch the swooping wolf. Moments later the cloudian clattered loudly down beside him, three triumphant children tumbling at his feet.

"We found a land below the circus," Liesel screamed.

"Its strange and grey, like a storm stopped still," went on Ferdie.

"Sound doesn't work in the same way there," panted Nate, "or time."

A dark look crossed the Wild Conductor's face.

"We saw Harper there," Liesel continued, "but she couldn't hear us no matter how hard we shouted."

The terribly tall man began to pace.

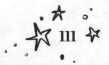

"Did the air feel empty of magic?" he asked. Ferdie nodded. "Was it swirling black and ghostly grey?" Now all the children nodded. "Did it seem like a dream a wolf might have in winter?" The children stared at him in surprise and the Wild Conductor began to describe the dream he'd been having ever since he was banished from the circus, and how

somewhere in that strange land he believed Star was trapped.

Nate cleared his throat. "We saw someone else there too," he uttered softly. The Wild Conductor stopped completely.

"She shimmered like smoke," said Ferdie, "until she heard a few notes of the cloudian, then she sort of ... well, glowed."

At this the tall man dropped to his knees, half in despair, half with relief. "It must be her – my Star," he half gasped. Then he hung his head. "How will we ever set her free without magic?"

Ferdie stepped forward and laid a hand on the tall man's shoulder. "Even in a circus of extraordinary things, there are forces stronger than magic," he said.

"Yes," Nate grinned, pulling the Wild Conductor to his feet.

"Like what?" said the tall man softly.

"Like love!" announced Liesel, completely amazing everyone. "Love is the way Harper was freed from the circus; it's the one thing that Othello Grande fears."

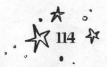

Everyone stared at her, dumbstruck. "You're right..." whispered the Wild Conductor, looking more alive than he had in days. And with that he gathered the boy with the serious scarf, the mouse-like girl who loved mischief and the boy with the wolf under the cluster of umbrellas to rest before they put their daring plan into action.

Chapter Eleven
THE STAR THAT COULD NOT SHINE

As dawn swept across the sky, a mist of marvels and mystery settled over the fields and sleepy village. High above the glistening whiteness, Harper came to a standstill. All around her circus folk were resting, getting a few moments of sleep before the big show later that morning.

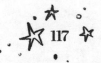

She'd had no luck finding her friends, and she sank down wearily beside the toffee apple stall and pulled the storm bloom from her pocket. Its lemony scent reminded her of home. As Harper examined its dusky grey petals, she noticed something odd. There was writing upon each petal, writing that Harper recognized, writing that spilled from the pencil of one of her best friends.

Harper, be brave!

This at once made her smile.

We are coming to save you. At midnight after the last show, go to the Heavens of the Circus. We will meet you there and tell you the rest of our brilliant plan!

Keep yours ears open for any stories you hear about a woman who glows like a star. She is somewhere trapped in the circus and we need to find her.

I'll explain all soon,

Love always,

The poet, the boy with the wolf, and the girl with a bird in her hair.

Harper sat bolt upright. *Star.* The word seemed to shine in her mind – the same word she'd seen etched in gold on a burnt poster. She opened the Scarlet Umbrella and crawled underneath it, pulling out the scroll of sheet music and the dazzling costume she'd found in the abandoned tent. It was quite clear now that the costume did indeed look like a star made of flames.

"A Fire Star," Harper murmured as she ran her eyes over the sheet music. The tune was bold and wonderful and filled with light and, even though Harper didn't know it, it sort of felt familiar. Then she noticed the signature of the composer at the bottom of the page and her heart froze.

In a dizzy blur Harper scrambled to her feet, closed the umbrella, scooped up Midnight and started to head to the back of the circus, towards the cobweb bridge. The strange grey land beneath the tents had left her with a creeping feeling in her stomach. But there was nothing else for it; if Harper wanted to find out what had happened to the Wild Conductor or who this mysterious glowing women was, she would have to face the figure with ember eyes.

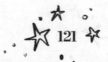

Midnight found the gap in the cloud quite quickly and before Harper had time to doubt herself they were climbing back down into the land below. At first Harper thought the tent was empty, but then shadows seemed to shimmer, and from within the gloom the figure emerged, her eyes flickering like candles.

Harper felt the impulse to run, but she made her feet still, forcing herself to smile. Midnight sprang into Harper's arms, tugging her piccolo flute from her pocket and pushing it into her hands. The world felt too still for music, but Harper began to play anyway – only the notes were incredibly hard to get out, each one taking almost all her breath as if she were playing the flute underwater.

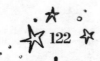

The figure's eyes seemed to brighten with hope. Harper closed her own eyes and thought only of the song, and the way her mother had learnt to sing underwater, pushing the notes out as much with her mind as her breath.

For a while the cloud seemed to fight her, swallowing away any sound she made, but Harper played on with every ounce of strength she had until finally the air started thinning, giving way to the song. Then every note came out in a rush, ringing through the sky. Both Harper and the figure with ember eyes

burst out laughing, and Harper noticed something extraordinary. The woman's heart was softly crackling like a low-burning fire and she was hovering just off the ground. Harper smiled and breathed one word: "Star."

"Yes," said the beautiful glowing woman in a lilting accent. As the song ceased, Star floated back to the ground, her eyes dancing with smiles. "You have a wondrous gift," she beamed, and Harper nodded shyly. But Star reached out and very delicately touched Harper's hand.

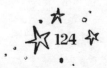

"No, you don't understand," she said. "For many years I have tried to glow, but my heart was so sad it could not shine. At first my friends visited, but no one could play their instrument through the mist. After many years of trying, they gave up, leaving me alone in my quiet, grey world. A girl with a heart of fire unable to shine."

Harper listened carefully. "So you are the Fire Star?" she asked and Star nodded. "Why do you stay here?" Harper cried.

"Othello Grande was so angry when I fell in love with his best friend that he banished me here. I can only leave if my heart glows, but music doesn't work here – so I am trapped," Star said breathlessly. "But with your music, perhaps I could escape."

Harper gave a nod of agreement. "And you will – my friends and I will see to that. But first tell me – what was the name of the musician you fell in love with?" said Harper, sounding very much like Ferdie.

"Professor Armoury," whispered Star. "Also known as the Wild Conductor."

Harper held her breath. Suddenly all of the tricks and schemes and twisted plans the Wild Conductor had used to try and win back his place in the Circus of Dreams made sense. It had all been to rescue Star from the wicked clutches of Othello Grande. Harper didn't dare tell Star the very man she had fallen in love with all of those years ago was somewhere just below the circus. Instead, she pulled her small golden harp out of the folds of the Scarlet Umbrella and beckoned Star deeper into the tent.

Chapter Twelve
THE GIRL WHO ESCAPED

Much, much later, when the sun had fully risen then slipped slowly through hours of daylight until it was ready to set again, Harper stood in a tent the colour of diamonds. The children's orchestra were just about to perform – for the sixth time that day. Harper and Midnight were completely exhausted, but they knew this was the last show before the rescue mission began.

At that very end of the show, all the storm-stirrers would head to the canteen tent to eat their supper, so Harper would need a good excuse to scuttle away to the Heavens of the Circus. It was going to be tricky but she would have to get her act wrong and then pretend to go and rehearse.

"Just stick with me boy – whatever happens," she whispered to Midnight, giving him a good-luck kiss. Harper was a little extra nervous about this show anyway, as her mum and dad were secretly watching.

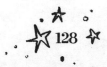

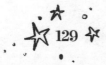

As the audience took their seats Harper climbed into the Scarlet Umbrella, set Midnight upon its brim, then rose into the air. The crowd gave an astounded gasp and, at the very back of the tent, Aurelia dabbed a proud tear from her eye and Hugo beamed lovingly. When Midnight started to play the piccolo flute, the crowd burst into peals of delighted laughter and Harper found herself laughing along. She leaped up on to the umbrella's silver handle in a single smooth bound and began to perform on her harp. The tempo quickened and the Scarlet Umbrella whirled around like a leaf on an autumn wind. A storm-stirrer swooped by, throwing Harper the bassoon. She gave it a loud honk and tossed it high. A cheer echoed up from below her, and Harper spread her arms like wings, waiting to catch the cymbals. She saw them come flying towards her. Her heart beat like thunder in her ears and Harper knew it was now or never. Even though it went against her every instinct she closed her eyes and let the cymbals clatter to the ground.

The crowd gasped and Harper leant backwards, falling delicately into the air. Storm-stirrers dived, seeming to come from every direction, catching the cat, the bassoon and the cymbals, but Harper slipped through their fingers, sailing down towards the crowds.

Hugo and Aurelia were both on their

feet, but in a flash of scarlet the umbrella spun upside down and caught Harper in its dome, knocking a few of the audience's hats off along the way. Then the umbrella swept around the tent collecting all the storm-stirrers, Midnight and the instruments until an entire circus troupe was balanced all over it. Then it hung perfectly still as if it had all been part of the act. The crowd could hardly contain their joy. Hugo and Aurelia could hardly contain their relief, and Harper could hardly contain her excitement, knowing she had the perfect excuse to miss supper.

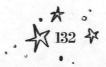

Harper raced to the Heavens of the Circus, where stars glittered, night birds sang softly to each other and three child-shaped shadows, along with one of a wolf, tiptoed hand in hand towards her. Harper ran at her friends in a bolt of happiness. "It's so good to see you," she laughed, flinging her arms around them.

"Great to see you too," grinned Ferdie, giving her a scarf-filled hug.

"Hope you've been enjoying life in the circus," grinned Nate, squeezing Harper's hand.

Liesel jumped up and down impatiently. "We need to tell you our brilliant plan – there's no time to lose."

Moments later all the children stood in a little line. Ferdie, Harper and Nate had bound their umbrellas together with edentwine, and they held them proudly in the air. Far below them in the sleepy village a church clock chimed midnight and Liesel gave her hair a wild shake. Storm awoke and shot into the sky, looping a ring around the moon and calling out a signal.

From within the swathes of starry cloud peddled the Wild Conductor, the cloudian spilling a melody across the sky. At once, Ferdie, Nate and Harper all began to play their instruments in the most awful manner – a racket of screaming strings, badly banged buttons and shrill shrieks on the harmonica – to cover the sound of the cloudian's lovely lullaby.

Liesel sprang into the back of the wolf, and after a small pat from Nate, Smoke bounded back into the circus, with Liesel pirouetting upon her silvery back as perfectly as any performer. At the sight of the wild beast and the dancing girl, storm-stirrers came rushing out of the canteen tent and formed a cheering crowd. Othello Grande put down his supper and barged his way roughly forwards, weighing up whether he thought Liesel and Smoke had enough talent to belong in his circus.

From high above the circus, the Wild Conductor glanced down and saw that Othello was occupied. He began to peddle harder so the magic of the cloudian's music softly took hold of the string of umbrellas and lifted them into the air, carrying Harper, Ferdie and Nate with them.

Ferdie reached out a hand and managed to pull himself down on to the back of the black bicycle, Harper and Nate gliding behind. Harper gave the Wild Conductor her biggest smile. She was out of the circus – she was almost free. Normally, no one ever escaped Othello Grande, but Harper had left once before so the magic couldn't hold her. Part one of the plan had worked

– now they just needed to get the Wild Conductor into the circus.

"Take the handlebars," said the tall man, giving Ferdie a wink. "Just steer straight for the fields below."

Ferdie gave him a serious salute and peddled on as the Wild Conductor climbed elegantly on to the thread of edentwine and walked along it like a tightrope, using the bright umbrellas as stepping stones. With one final long-legged bound, he sailed through the night and landed softly in the Heavens of the Circus, checking all around before removing his hat and turning his satin coat inside out. He raised part of it over his head like a hood, covering his magpie-feather hair so he was quite unrecognizable. Othello, who was still watching Liesel, would never know it was him.

Then he took a large gulp of air, as if the night might give him courage as he set off through the Circus of Dreams. The circus that was once his home; the circus in which Star was trapped. This time nothing would stop him.

So he didn't see that, high on the horizon, Harper and Nate had quietly switched umbrellas. Harper now held a dark grey umbrella, while Nate and

Midnight rode beneath the Scarlet Umbrella. As both children tucked their legs up, they looked almost the same. In fact, it was impossible to tell them apart.

Chapter Thirteen
STRANGE ORCHESTRA

In the centre of the Circus of Dreams, Liesel and Smoke were putting on such a wonderful show that Othello really was charmed by their skill. He loomed towards them with a sly grin and Liesel knew they didn't have long. She couldn't risk getting trapped in the circus as well. Gritting her teeth, and hoping that her friends had had enough time to escape, she gave the wolf a little nudge with her foot.

Sharp, silver jaws snapped open, white teeth gleamed in the moonlight and, with an ear-splitting snarl, the wolf pounced, knocking Othello Grande clean off his feet. Everyone in the circus went rigid with fear. The only sound that could be heard was the clang and clatter of badly played music. Then, to Liesel's horror, the glorious tune of the cloudian came pattering by on the breeze.

Othello struggled ungracefully to his feet, the wolf long forgotten, his beady eyes scanning the sky for the cloudian. With a snap of fingers, one of his eagles swooped down and he dived on to its back, soaring up towards the silhouette of the black bicycle and the trail of bright umbrellas.

"No one escapes from my circus," Othello boomed, hovering on the white-winged bird as he glared at the children. Ferdie started to peddle for all he was worth, trying to get away, but it was no use. The bird's snapping beak grabbed the Scarlet Umbrella and snatched it away, ripping the unbreakable edentwine and circling back to the circus.

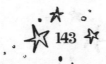

Ferdie peered up at Harper, who was curled beneath the grey umbrella, and gave her a serious wink. As Othello's bird swooped away, Harper dived through the night and on to the back of the bike. She quickly unfastened the twine, setting the grey umbrella

free, so it could drift down to the fields below. Then together, Ferdie and Harper cycled towards the land beneath the circus, a melody of mid-winter moons and snowy forests ringing through the clouds.

In the Heavens of the Circus, the powerful bird tossed the Scarlet Umbrella down. Othello's cackle blasted the night, but then very abruptly his laughter rattled to a stop. The child beneath the umbrella was not Harper. It was a boy with skin smooth as night, holding a harmonica. How could he have been so foolish?

"Where is she?" Othello bellowed, shaking Nate roughly by the shoulders.

"She's safe in the village," Nate replied breezily, pointing way down below at the grey umbrella nestled in the rolling fields.

Confusion clouded Othello Grande's small eyes. "But how did she get out of my circus?" He scowled, his mind slowly beginning to work out exactly who Harper was. "The girl who escaped..." he breathed. Nate gave a simple nod and the furious ringmaster cast him aside, shoving him dangerously close to edge of the Heavens of the Circus.

Nate gave a long low whistle and with a magnificent bound Smoke appeared, still carrying Liesel.

Othello backed away from the wolf's snapping jaws.

"We have to go to the land below the circus," Liesel whispered to Nate as she slipped lightly off of Smoke's back. "Midnight can lead the way."

The two children, the cat and the wolf darted away without so much as a backwards glance at the red-bearded ringmaster. Othello's eyebrows knitted into a huge thundery frown, and he strode after the children.

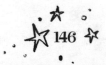

By the time Nate, Liesel, Midnight and Smoke reached the gap in the cloud, the entire circus was following. The cobweb bridge swayed beneath the weight of so many feet. The circus troupe shivered as they felt the coldness of the air, and took in the fog-like cloud that swirled around them, slowing time and whispering silence. Some of them had been here before, long ago. But others didn't even know this place existed, and were startled to see the tombstone-coloured tent rising out of the shadows like the towers of a haunted castle.

"Who lives here?" breathed Skylar, but at that moment her question was answered.

A figure with sparkling eyes stepped from the tent. She was the most enchanting person Liesel had ever seen, a vision of shimmering smoke and glittering sparks.

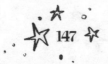

Nate could feel her incredible warmth and something else, like the crackling of excitement before a bonfire, and with a small grin Nate realized that this strange dark land no longer felt empty of magic. It felt charged with power and hope.

"Raise your instruments and follow me," came a voice the children recognized, and they both broke into a cheer. For there amidst the dream of winter stood a man in a black satin coat. A man who was a far better conductor than Othello Grande could ever hope to be. A man whose music could set your heart on fire.

The Wild Conductor's hands were trembling. He hardly dared look at the woman with ember eyes. Instead, he put his energy into the song, holding his conductor's wand as if it were magical and conducting the entire circus. Those who had instruments raised them up; others opened their mouths to sing, while the storm-stirrers got ready leap and spin. Yet, to everyone's astonishment, no sound came out. It just seemed to vanish into the cold dreamy mist.

"Ha," came a mean voice from above.

The cobweb bridge shuddered as Othello came crashing down it. But he laughed darkly when he saw the confused crowd in front of him.

"So, you thought you'd rescue your precious Star, did you?" He snorted, laughing rudely at the Wild Conductor.

"Yes," answered the Wild Conductor in a steady voice. "And that's exactly what I will do. You can't keep her trapped in a dream of winter for ever."

Othello wrinkled his nose, rather like a big pig. "I can do whatever I like," he whined. "It's my circus – I cast the spells and none of them can ever be broken."

The Wild Conductor frowned deeply, then waved his wand high. His odd orchestra strained to play their instruments, but still no sound came out. Othello chuckled cruelly. The figure with ember eyes held his gaze, her head high and proud.

Then they heard it: a gentle plucking of strings, as soft as a wish. It was the unmistakeable sound of a harp.

A girl with dark hair and sea-grey eyes appeared upon a drift of silver-lined cloud, which formed the top of the cloudian. On the bike below, Ferdie peddled with everything he had, and the air around them quivered. Othello turned white with fury as a flurry of musical raindrops and harp music filled the sky.

"Join in!" beamed Nate, tooting away on the harmonica. Liesel seized her gleaming violin, Rat grabbed a bassoon, and Skylar used Harper's maracas, which she shook and played as she cartwheeled wildly. The entire circus followed; coins were jingled, hats became drums, and an old boot was used as a trumpet. People laughed and

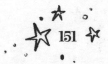

sang and clapped and whooped and the grey mist began to roll away, leaving only a land of night-coloured clouds.

The little crowd were so busy following the Wild Conductor that none of them noticed the effect the music had on Star. She began to glow faintly like a red ember, then a cool blue flame: quiet, but very alive. A white spark fell from her chest and she gave a light laugh as her arms opened like wings and her feet rose from the ground. Up she floated, up towards the cloudian like a fairground lantern, her heart beginning to dazzle.

Chapter Fourteen
THE FIRE STAR

One moment the sky was full of night, the next it was full of fire, as Star and Othello Grande collided. She dropped her cloak and came at the ringmaster, spinning through the sky like a Catherine wheel, a crackling burst of colourful flames.

Harper was speechless. Star really did

look magical – a girl who needed no tightrope or strings or wings. She simply shone.

From beyond the thinning mist, Ferdie saw everything. He desperately wanted to reach for his pencil and scribble down a poem, but he had to keep his mind focused on peddling. Liesel was beside herself with glee, loving every fiery moment, while Nate was caught in a state of wild wonderment.

"I thought I put your light out for good," yelled Othello, as the heat from Star forced him backwards.

Star swirled in the air, her heart a crest of brilliant sparks. "You tried to put out my light," she said, and though her voice was gentle, it rang out as clear as nightingales. "You tricked us," she continued. "You promised the Wild Conductor that if he left the circus I would be safe. But you lied."

At this, all of the music stopped, even the harp. Nobody dared to breathe. You could have dropped a button from the moon and heard it splash in the stream below.

"Yes I did," agreed Othello smugly. "Then I cast a spell so the Wild Conductor could never return," he boasted, "and I imprisoned you in the land below."

There was an angry uproar from the performers. The Wild Conductor turned to Star, his face grave with sorrow. "I tried again and again to rejoin the circus," he stuttered.

"And I tried to glow," she explained sadly. "I thought if you saw my light you might find me. But until now there was only ash."

"Ha," laughed Othello. "Serves you right. No one gets to choose their heart's wish in my circus."

Liesel's eyes glittered with rage. What an awful man Othello was! She wasn't going to stand for it. She pulled off one of her shoes and hurled it at his head. With a clunk, it hit him and he wailed in a way that shook the stars.

"How dare you!" Othello screamed, blaming the Wild Conductor. The tall man held up his conductor's wand to defend himself, but Othello was too fast, and with a swing he sent the Wild Conductor wheeling across the sky, where Ferdie managed to catch him on the back of the cloudian.

But as the tall man landed wonkily on the black bicycle, Ferdie was catapulted into the air. He flew upwards in a gloriously poetic arc and whacked straight into Othello Grande's face. Star shot forwards like a shooting star and caught Ferdie on her shoulders, careful not to singe him with her glowing heart. There was a scuffle and a shout, and then Othello found himself overbalancing, plummeting down towards the sleepy village below. Everyone closed their eyes in horror. Everyone except Harper. For, even though Othello had done terrible things, he didn't deserve this. With a clear thought, she summoned the Scarlet Umbrella out of Nate's back pocket and jumped into it, racing down to catch the huge man by his foot.

The sight of Othello swinging back and forth like an upside-down elephant was enough to make everyone laugh.

"Let me go, you wretch." Othello seethed, but Harper could tell he didn't mean it – his voice was wobbling.

"I will let you go," she said softly, "so long as you promise to leave the circus for ever."

Othello went silent with fear. But what

choice did he have? With a furious nod, he agreed.

To Harper's surprise the scarlet silk was unbelievably strong and didn't so much as strain beneath the enormous weight. She set Othello down inside the abandoned tent and drew back.

"You'll never keep me away from the circus," he growled, but even as he spoke, his circus were hurrying away back up the cobweb bridge until all that were left were Star, the Wild Conductor, Harper, her parents, and three other children from the City of Clouds.

"I wouldn't be so sure about that," said Nate calmly. He bent to whisper to his beautiful wolf, and with a single bite her teeth sliced through the cobweb bridge so its strands of ancient spider silk fell away. Othello could do nothing but stare in horror as the strange wintery land was cut free from the circus and, ever so slowly, swirled away.

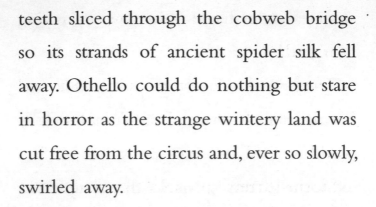

Harper was safely in her Scarlet Umbrella with Midnight and Liesel. Ferdie was back on the black bicycle with the Wild Conductor. Hugo and Aurelia were settled on top of the cloudian's silver-lined cloud, and Star was hovering in the air, her heart ablaze. As the last strands of the bridge fell away she lifted Nate and the wolf out of the land below and carried them to the safety of the Circus of Dreams. Othello could do nothing but stare in fury as the strange, wintery land drifted away, carrying him with it.

The last anyone saw of him was his red beard, a splash of colour against the grey world he had created.

Storm-stirrers appeared like a silent sea of feathers and began to create an almighty storm. The Circus of Dreams was moving on, travelling far from the abandoned tent. Thunder and lightning struck, snowflakes danced, rainbows rose and vanished and, as a shower of sparkling sleet fell, the spell that bound the circus lifted and it was finally free.

Chapter Fifteen
A CIRCUS SET FREE

I'm not sure if you ever have seen a circus set free, but imagine a fairground carousel that suddenly comes to life, all its bright horses galloping away with wild hearts, and that will be close. Harper stood between Hugo and Aurelia with Midnight perched on her shoulder. Ferdie and Liesel were tumbling about with the storm-stirrers. Star and the Wild Conductor were standing a little way apart from each other, talking shyly. And Nate was with the lightning-leader – and his bright-eyed wolf.

"What will become of the circus now?" asked Harper quietly.

Liesel sprang into the air. "The Wild Conductor can run it," she yipped, gesturing boldly at the terrifyingly tall man. But, to everyone's amazement, the tall man shook his head.

"For many years I chased the circus across the world," he said with a gentleness the children had never heard before, "but the only person I wanted to find was Star."

As he spoke, Star turned to smile at

him, her heart glowing, her feet hovering just off the ground. "Then let's forget the circus and travel together," she beamed. "You can play your cloudian and I will dance through the sky."

The Wild Conductor looked as if he could burst with happiness. "Whatever you wish," he managed to utter, and Ferdie was sure he saw him wipe a tear from his eye.

There were murmurs that rippled through the crowd as soft as waves. What would become of the circus now?

The lightning-leader stood tall, blue electricity crackling through her hair, making her look quite marvellous. "The Circus of Dreams belongs to all of us," she said in a voice like deep velvet. "We are what make it and we will run it together, writing new rules, finding a new path. As long as we have storms, we can sail through the skies." The other members touched their hearts and nodded.

But Aurelia stepped forwards. "This wonderful place has been our home for many years," she said in her sea-salt voice.

Hugo nodded. "But we would like

to have some time with our beloved daughter," he explained. "We don't want to leave the circus for ever, just spend some time as a family."

Everyone smiled as they realized that this was now possible. And so, by the light of the moon, a new set of circus rules were written, a set that everyone agreed with. People could come and go with the seasons, families could visit, and performers could follow their heart's desire wherever it might lead them. It would still be a circus of wonders and wishes, but this time the dream would belong to everyone, and that would be the real magic.

There was only one thing left to do – and that was celebrate. The entire troupe sprang into a giddy display of dancing and singing and acrobatic tricks as fabulous as the most fearsome of storms. When the moon and stars began to fade and sunlight trickled across the sky, the children saw that the circus had drifted back to the City of Clouds – the city they loved so much, floating like a vision of a dream above the Tall Apartment Block.

The children, the Wild Conductor and all of the circus folk climbed down the rope ladder on to the rooftop, marvelling at their newfound freedom. Great Aunt Sassy came rushing out to greet them. "My darling Harper," she wept, sweeping Harper into a lavender-scented hug. "I thought I had lost you."

Elsie Caraham at once offered Star and the Wild Conductor her patch of the rooftop to live on, and with the help of the storm-stirrers, they fetched a spare silver-bright tent from the circus and pitched it on the roof of the Tall Apartment Block. It looked quite peculiar, but strangely wonderful too.

Skylar and Isabella at once became friends, and Skylar agreed to stay with the Lucas family and teach Isabella some circus tricks, so she may one day join the circus too.

Hugo and Aurelia – well, they decided to make their home in the unforgotten concert hall in the basement. There was plenty of room for Harper, Midnight and

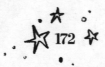

Ruby-Mischief, the little sharp-clawed cat they had managed to secretly keep in the circus. Though Harper would still often stay with her wonderful, hat-loving Great Aunt Sassy, in the little flat she had grown up in.

After a day of new beginnings and fast-forming friendships, summer-dew rain came splashing from the sky and the Circus of Dreams sailed away on a storm. Harper, Ferdie, Nate and Liesel stood on the rooftop waving. It really had been an extraordinary adventure.

Liesel frowned crossly. "I really wanted to run away with the circus," she sulked.

Ferdie ruffled his sister's hair fondly "I know... So did I," he agreed, "but there's always next year."

Harper took Liesel's hand. "And don't forget, some of the circus are here anyway."

The four of them turned away from the sky and looked across the roof of their home. There was Star teaching Skylar how to cartwheel over a cloud. The Wild Conductor, furiously composing a new song. Great Aunt Sassy, stitching a wondrous new apron for Hugo to wear when he opened his biscuit stall.

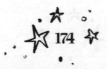

Liesel grinned. "I suppose The Tall Apartment Block is pretty special." She giggled, and with that the boy with the wolf, the girl with the Scarlet Umbrella, the boy with the serious scarf and the girl with the sleeping bird in her hair crowded down the stairwells to Harper's little flat to sip hot lavender syrup and murmur about the magical rescue they had all been part of.

Later that night, when clocks all over the City of Clouds chimed twelve, all of the children were still wide awake, tucked up safe in their beds, their hearts still light with adventure.

Ferdie sat up scribbling a poem. His first about love. Liesel was busy planning a circus act of a thousand dancing mice. Nate lay curled with his starry-eyed wolf, so grateful that together they had found a bridge no one else could see – a spider-silk path that led to the land below.

Harper lay in a hammock of sequins in the unforgotten concert hall – her home for the winter. Midnight purred peacefully on her lap, and she gasped to herself with wonder. The circus was finally free and her parents were really here – in the Tall Apartment Block, with her as she had always dreamed they would be, but never quite dared to believe. "The Wild Conductor was right," she whispered to Midnight. "Love really is strong enough to defy magic." And as she thought of the silver tent on the rooftop, she smiled. The Fire Star was glowing once more and the Wild Conductor was finally happy, and that seemed like the most magical thing in all the world.

As Harper snuggled down, she was sure she could hear the music of the cloudian spilling across the rain-filled skies. With a happy thought she closed the Scarlet Umbrella – even magical umbrellas need to rest between adventures – then tucked her golden harp beneath her pillow and cuddled Midnight close. It was time for a different sort of adventure, one that was full of family and friendship, music and cats, stories and songs and just a sprinkling of magic, right here in the Tall Apartment Block. As Harper's mind filled with dazzling thoughts of all that was to come, she drifted into a deep and lovely sleep.

As Harper slept she dreamed of flying, floating in the Scarlet Umbrella through a sky full of swirling melodies. She saw the circus in all its wild splendour and knew one day she and Midnight would help lead it. She saw many more musical instruments that

she would create: a violin shaped like a heart that you play with a feather; a flute that could conjure a rainbow; an underwater piano that played the sounds of the sea. Harper saw herself travelling to a thousand different places, with her friends at her side, filling people's hearts with music and droplets of wonder as gentle as rain.

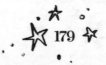

Also look out for . . .

HARPER AND THE Scarlet Umbrella

When every single cat in the City of Clouds goes missing, Harper is determined to find her beloved Midnight and all the other precious pets.

Harper can't believe her luck when she discovers a magic flying umbrella and with the help of all her friends she sets off on a rescue adventure.

But they're up against the powerful Wild Conductor... Will they manage to bring the cats home?

Turn the page to read the beginning of this book.

Chapter One
THE BROKEN UMBRELLA

From the fourteenth floor of the Tall Apartment Block, Harper gazed dreamily across the City of Clouds. Trams rumbled through heavy rain and bright umbrellas bobbed like little boats.

"Darling, I'm leaving with the Dutch Opera House in ten minutes sharp," Great

Aunt Sassy cooed, as she stitched a pink petticoat into a gorgeous twirly gown. "They're picking me up by helicopter."

Harper smiled and put her arms around her Great Aunt Sassy's large waist, the

scent of lavender tickling her nose. Sassy Miller was the chief dressmaker for the Dutch Opera House. It was her job to sew hems, knit hats and create fabulous dresses.

Every four weeks, when the moon was round and full, Great Aunt Sassy travelled to Holland to check on all her beautiful gowns. Harper secretly liked it when Great Aunt Sassy went away, as she got to stay with the other residents of the Tall Apartment Block. Tonight she was staying with strange old Elsie Caraham, who lived on the topmost floor. Tomorrow she was with Madame Flora at the ballet school, on floor three.

The sound of a whirring helicopter filled

the little flat. "My ride has arrived!" Great Aunt Sassy cheered, seizing her suitcase and charging out the door.

Harper ran to catch up with her, grabbing her yellow umbrella as she went. As they stepped on to the rooftop a Heartbeat of rain drummed from the sky. Harper hardly noticed. In the City of Clouds it rained every day, in many different ways, pouring down water that was good enough to drink.

There was:

Summer Dew: a light rain that barely touched you.

Sea Mist: a soft rain which emerged from the air like fog.

Heartbeat: an even rain, steady as your heart.

Cloudburst: a downpour that soaked you to the skin.

Icefall: a hard rain that struck like hail.

Thunder Break: when the sky was alive with storms.

"Have a weekend as wonderful as you," Sassy beamed, kissing Harper's forehead and struggling into the helicopter.

"I will," Harper giggled, her mind already skipping at the thought of the fun she was going to have.

But as the helicopter span into the clouds, the force from its propellers snatched Harper's yellow umbrella and tossed it into the air. Harper gave a squeal as it was thrown in a puddle at her feet, badly torn.

From the sky above, Great Aunt Sassy peered down and almost dropped her teacup.

"Whatever will we do?" she groaned. "Everyone in the City of Clouds owns an umbrella and now Harper's is ruined." She leaned through the swathes of swirling cloud, took a deep breath and then – knowing that Harpers life would change for ever – called, "Darling, you must use the Scarlet Umbrella. It was left to you by..."

But Great Aunt Sassy's words were stolen away by the wind. Harper was alone, a little girl on a rooftop with a broken umbrella.

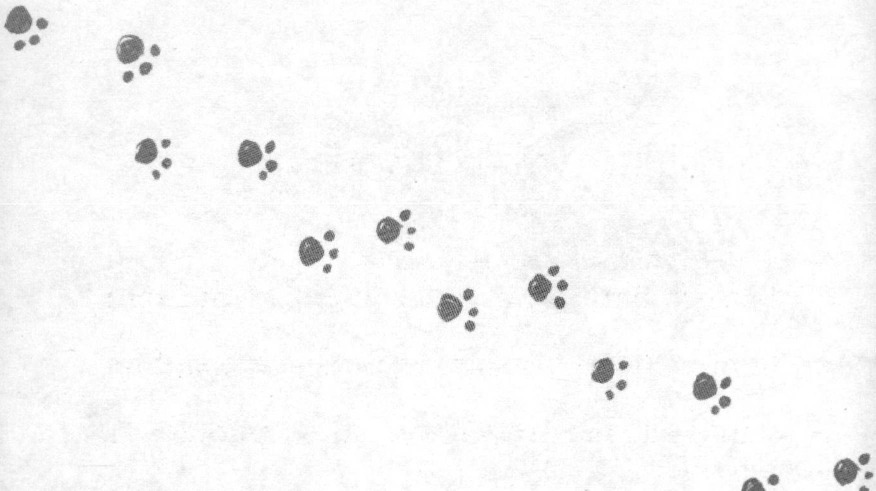

Chapter Two
THE BIRDCAGE

Harper blinked in amazement as the rain lightened to a soft Summer Dew. She stared at her reflection in a puddle. A girl with pale skin, dark hair and eyes the colour of a winter sea gazed back at her with a big smile. "I can use the Scarlet Umbrella," Harper gasped.

She darted down the stairs, through the door of their little flat and into the bathroom. A shiver of excitement danced over Harper's skin. In the corner of the bathroom stood an enormous birdcage. Locked inside its slim white bars was an umbrella of magnificent scarlet silk.

So often had Harper dreamed of opening the birdcage, but Great Aunt Sassy had never allowed her to, insisting that the Scarlet Umbrella was too old and fragile to use. Carefully, Harper picked up a tiny golden key which hung above the sink. It had been there for as long as Harper could remember, shining through her memories like a key to forgotten secrets. Gently she turned the key and with a click the birdcage was open. Harper held her breath and lifted the umbrella out. It burst open in her hands, making her jump and laugh all at once! It really was quite splendid – like a prop from one of Great Aunt Sassy's operas. "It weighs nothing at

all," Harper smiled, for it felt as if she was holding a handful of feathers, and though it was very old, the umbrella didn't seem fragile at all.

"Midnight!" Harper yelled, tearing around the little flat. "Midnight, come and see my amazing umbrella."

But Midnight was nowhere to be found. Harper pulled a small piccolo flute from her pocket and played Midnight's favourite melody. But still he did not appear. She peeked beneath the table and noticed something very odd. Midnight's bowl of cream and peppermint mouse had not been touched. A whisper of worry crept into Harper's heart.

You see, Midnight wasn't quite like any

other cat. Five years ago, on the night of the Fearsome Storm, he had mysteriously arrived at the stroke of twelve. The name had seemed perfect.

Midnight had mint-green eyes and jet-black fur with snow-white paws and a white-tipped tail. Wherever Harper wandered, Midnight would follow, three paces behind. Sometimes when Great Aunt Sassy took Harper to the ballet or to the cinema,

Midnight would already be there, curled happily in Harper's seat. How he guessed where she was going to sit, nobody ever knew.

Harper stood in the middle of the flat, breathing in the scent of lavender and listening to a lullaby of sad Summer Dew rain. And suddenly Harper felt terribly lonely. "Where are you, Midnight?" she whispered … and that's when the magical thing happened.

Also look out for . . .

HARPER AND THE Circus of Dreams

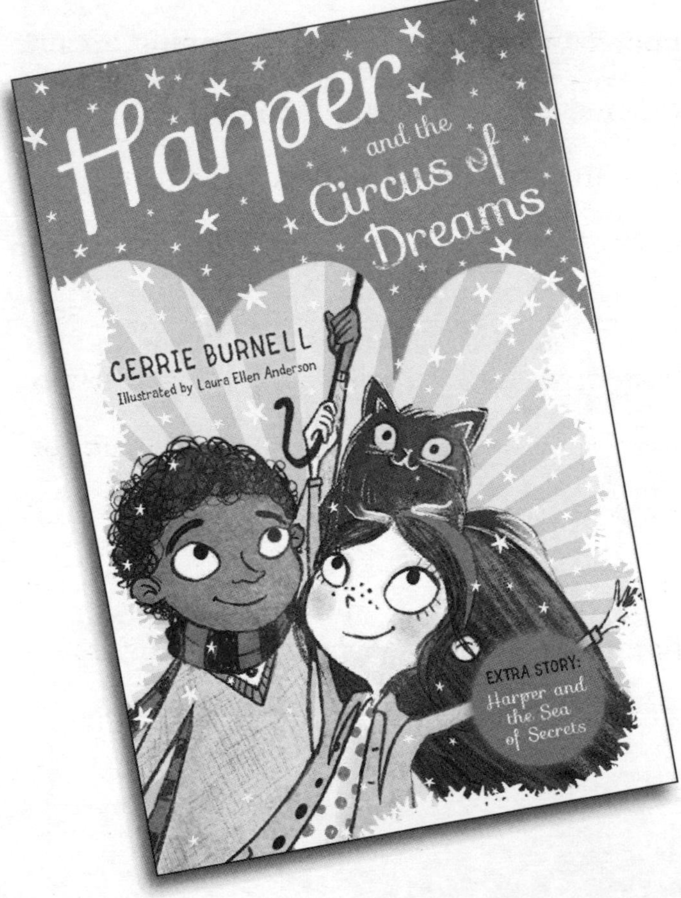

Late one evening as the stars begin to twinkle, Harper and her friends are flying on the scarlet umbrella when they see a girl running on air, skipping along a tightrope. She leads them to the Circus of Dreams, suspended in the air by hot air balloons. As the children meet the spectacular circus baker, the sea-singer, the mysterious fortune teller and the acrobatics troop, they begin to realise something about Harper's past...

Turn the page to read the beginning of this book.

Chapter One
A HOWLING WOLF

From the rooftop of the Tall Apartment Block, Harper perched beneath her Scarlet Umbrella and gazed down at the City of Clouds. Sea-Mist rain filled the air, and twilight swept across the sky, turning the raindrops the colour of smoke. Everything was peaceful.

Her beloved cat, Midnight, purred around her ankles, his green eyes twinkling. Harper raised her bow and began to softly play her viola. A single hopeful note rang out before a fierce howling filled the air. Harper dropped her bow and stared around her. There, at the other end of the rooftop, was a wolf the colour of dusk, and a boy lurking in the shadows.

Most children would be terrified of seeing a wolf on their roof. Most children would run and scream with fear. But most children weren't best friends with Nate Nathanielson.

Nate was a boy who lived on the tenth floor. He had found the wolf as a cub, given her a home and named her Smoke.

Smoke loved Nate as if they were part of a pack, and her star-bright eyes could see all the things that Nate could not. She wasn't a guide dog, or a guard dog, or a creature you could you call a pet. She was a wild companion, with wisdom in her heart and the full moon in her howl. But tonight something seemed to be troubling her.

Harper lifted her bow and played three sharp notes – the secret signal to summon her friends. There was a stirring of leaves and a pattering of light feet as a small, mouse-like girl flitted across the roof and threw her arms around the wolf.

"Hello, Liesel," Harper said with a smile, ruffling the small girl's knotted hair.

Liesel, who had large eyes and a love of fairy-tale witches, buried her face in the wolf's silvery coat, trying to soothe her.

The sound of serious footsteps echoed across the roof. "Hi, Ferdie," called Nate, recognizing the sound of his friend's footfall. Ferdie – Liesel's older brother – came hurrying over, still scribbling the last line of a poem. He tightened his scarf, tucked his pencil behind his ear and said, in a serious voice, "I think Smoke's howling at something in the sky."

The others squinted up. Yet all they saw were thickening clouds and the glint of evening starlight.

"It's too dark," moaned Liesel.

Harper gave her a smile. "What we need," she beamed, "is to fly!"

The children sprang into action. Nate pulled a strand of edentwine from his pocket and fastened Midnight's cat basket to the Scarlet Umbrella's handle. With a wild-eyed grin, Liesel shot into the basket. Ferdie grabbed a strand of twine and attached a big wooden kite to the umbrella's spike, then wove his arms through the kite's bars like a hang-glider. Harper winked at Midnight, who jumped on to her head, landing like a little furry hat. Nate gave a low whistle and, with a breathtaking bound, Smoke pounced on the umbrella's scarlet dome.

Harper and Nate both clasped the

umbrella's handle closely. "Ready?" Harper whispered.

"Ready!" the others called.

"Up!" she cried, and the Scarlet Umbrella soared into the sky, taking the four children, the cat and the wolf with it. The flickering lights of the City of Clouds vanished far below, and the children held their breath as they sailed towards the moon.

Up and up they raced, as if they were lighter than autumn leaves. Liesel leaned out of the cat basket and gave a shriek of joy. The inky sky made her feel like dancing. Ferdie laughed as the Scarlet Umbrella dipped through a fog of silken cloud, his mind filling with a million

stories. Nate was silent, straining to hear what his wolf might have sensed, and feeling the world shift around him.

Harper kept her eyes closed, for beyond the howl of the wolf and the purr of her cat, she thought she heard music. Just for a moment her heart seemed to tremble, for there was the tune that haunted her dreams – the one she could never quite play. Then they swirled upwards and the song vanished, leaving the world strangely still.

The umbrella hung in darkness, like a red boat on a deep and silent sea. Liesel coughed and giggled, Ferdie fiddled with his scarf, and Harper wondered what sort of cloud this might be, for it didn't look like any of the ones that usually floated above the city. Nate carefully uncurled one hand and ran his fingers through the rain. "There's a storm coming," he whispered.

"A storm?" asked Harper, taking in the stillness of the deep night sky.

Nate shrugged. "Yes. There's something stirring up the wind, mixing everything together. I can feel it."

"But what?" pondered Ferdie, reaching out to touch a drop of moonlight.

Something shot past Liesel like a dart of ice and feathers, and she gave a sudden gasp. "There's someone in the clouds," she squealed. "A ghost in the fog!"

None of the children really believed in

ghosts, yet as they craned their eyes into the dark they saw a girl moving faster than lightning. A girl who seemed to be running on air.

Chapter Two
THE STORY OF THE FEARSOME STORM

"What is it?" asked Nate, who could sense the amazement that gripped his friends.

The others did their best to describe what they could see. "Somewhere within the mist is a girl in a cloak of snow," began Ferdie.

"Her skin is golden brown," said Harper as she watched the girl leap between clouds as easily if they were stepping stones.

"She's got plaits that are full of lightning," piped up Liesel, who was now balancing on top of the cat basket on one foot, trying to get a better look at this wondrous cloud-skipping girl.

Nate opened his mouth to say something, but at that moment thunder bellowed like a bear, and the Scarlet Umbrella was thrown across the sky.

"Hold on!" cried Harper as a whirl of wind that sang like birds whooshed past, filling their heads with harmonies.

"We need to turn the umbrella over," shouted Nate as the singing grew louder.

No sooner had Nate spoken than the umbrella spun upside down by itself, catching Harper, Midnight and Nate, and somehow tipping in the wolf too. Ferdie and Liesel screamed as the kite and cat basket collided, and then their mouths fell open as a rainbow of night colours appeared before them. It was the strangest storm the children had ever seen.

Harper gathered her thoughts and, ignoring the song of the storm, she commanded the umbrella to return to the Tall Apartment Block.

As they scrambled back on to the roof Liesel gave a little yelp. "Look at the Scarlet Umbrella," she cried, pointing to a glistening row of icicles that hung from its bright-red edge.

"And Smoke's fur is full of stars," grinned Nate, putting the tiny glittering fragments carefully in his pocket.

"Midnight's covered in tufts of winter sky," giggled Harper.

"What a super storm," sighed Ferdie, "but who on earth is the girl in the sky?"

"And why could we hear birds singing?" wondered Harper, removing a feather that was caught behind Nate's ear.

"Can we keep the girl in the sky a secret?" Liesel begged.

The children nodded gleefully. For there was nothing more exciting than a secret shared.

The residents of the Tall Apartment Block came hurrying over to help untangle the edentwine. "We haven't seen a storm as good as this for at least five years!" said Elsie Caraham merrily. Elsie was the oldest resident of the Tall Apartment Block and she remembered everything.

"The skies haven't been so alive since the night of the Fearsome Storm," agreed Harper's Great Aunt Sassy.

Everyone smiled, including Harper. She knew exactly why the Fearsome Storm was special and she loved hearing the tale. "Tell us the story again, Great Aunt Sassy," Harper pleaded as they made their way indoors.

When everyone was gathered inside Harper and Great Aunt Sassy's little flat with a mug of hot cocoa, Sassy began the story. "Five years ago, on the night of the Fearsome Storm, a little girl with dark hair and sea-grey eyes appeared on the rooftop."

"Wow," breathed Liesel, who loved

the mystery that surrounded Harper's arrival, and wished with all her heart it had happened to her.

"A little girl clasping a Scarlet Umbrella," added Isabella, a member of the Lucas family from the seventh floor.

"Nobody knew where she'd come from, or how she'd ended up on the roof," said Peter, Ferdie and Liesel's father. "The only clue was a letter, which was pinned to the Scarlet Umbrella by the feather of a dove."

"What did the note say?" asked Ferdie, who knew the answer already but wanted to hear it again.

Great Aunt Sassy swept across the flat and opened a little drawer. Carefully, she pulled out a crumpled piece of paper, winked warmly at Harper and read the note.

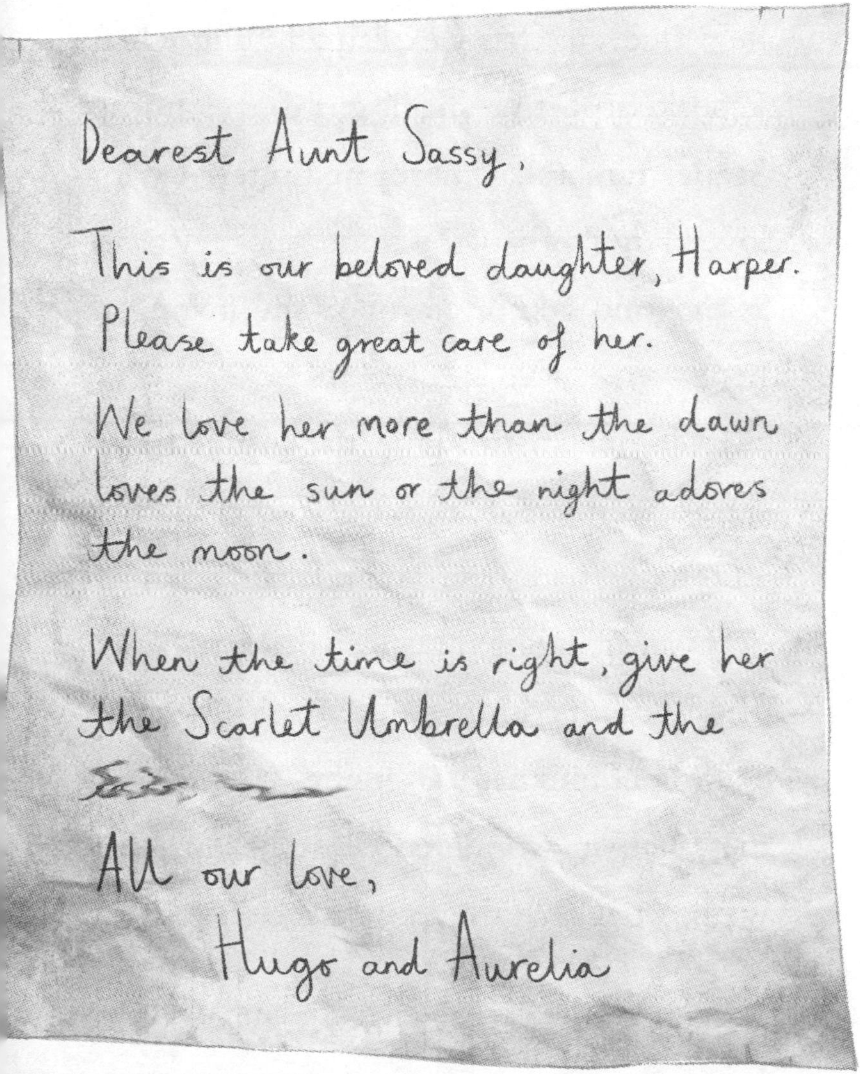

Dearest Aunt Sassy,

This is our beloved daughter, Harper.
Please take great care of her.
We love her more than the dawn
loves the sun or the night adores
the moon.

When the time is right, give her
the Scarlet Umbrella and the
[illegible]

All our love,
Hugo and Aurelia

Nobody knew what the last word said as it had been smudged by a raindrop.

"I hadn't seen my nephew Hugo since he was seven," Sassy explained. "But when I peeked at the small girl beneath the Scarlet Umbrella, my heart fluttered with love. For she had the same sea-grey eyes as me, and I knew at once she belonged here.

Everyone in the little flat grinned and sipped their cocoa. For it was true, Harper and Sassy had been wonderfully happy ever since, living in an apartment block of music and costumes and stories and cats.

Sometimes late at night, it was true that Harper wondered who her parents were, or where they might be. But with

Midnight to keep her company and the residents of the Tall Apartment Block watching over her, she rarely felt sad about it. It was only when she heard her star-song that thoughts of her family danced across her dreams, with a sadness she couldn't quite shake.

Cerrie Burnell is a presenter and writer, best known for her work in children's TV, and she featured in the *Guardian*'s 2011 list of 100 most inspirational women. Her other titles in this same series include *Harper and the Scarlet Umbrella*, *Harper and the Circus of Dreams*, *Harper and the Sea of Secrets (A World Book Day 2016 book)* and *Harper and the Night Forest*.

Laura Ellen Anderson is the incredibly talented illustrator of the *John Smith Is Not Boring* series, the *Witch Wars* series, the *Swashbuckle Lil* series as well as all the other *Harper* titles. She is also the creator of *Evil Emperor Penguin* and *Amelia Fang*.

Picture books by the same creators:

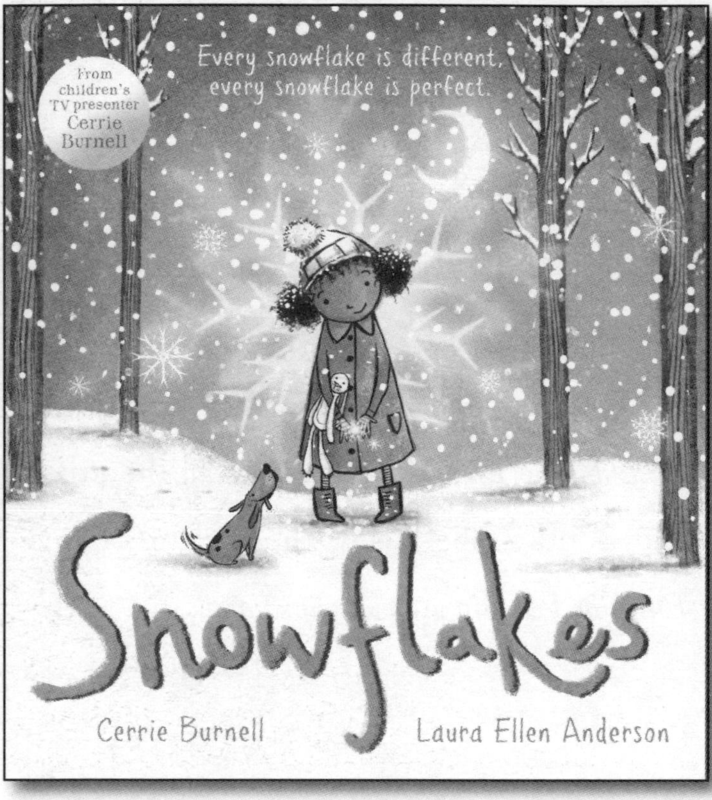
Every snowflake is different,
every snowflake is perfect.
From children's TV presenter Cerrie Burnell
Snowflakes
Cerrie Burnell
Laura Ellen Anderson

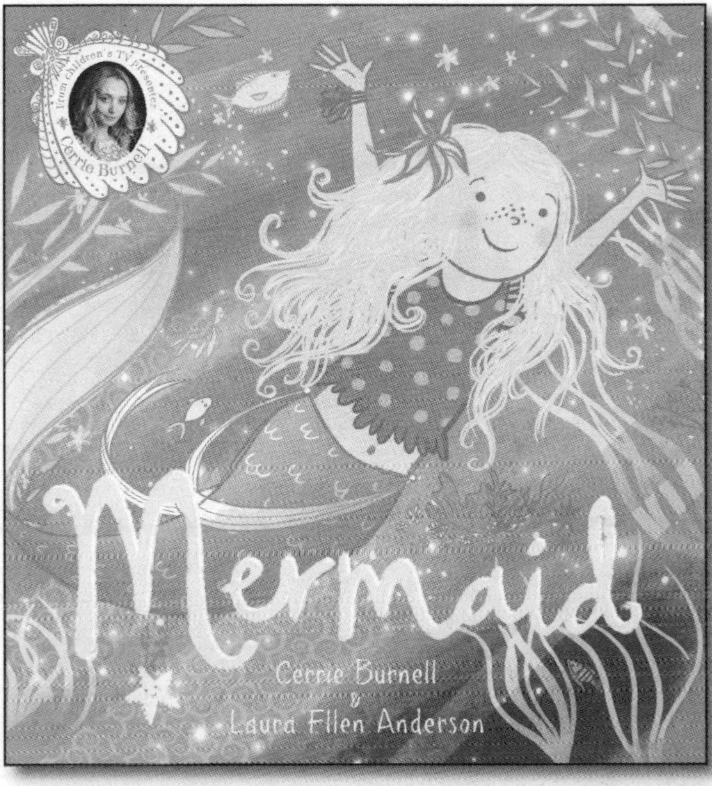
From children's TV presenter
Cerrie Burnell
Mermaid
Cerrie Burnell
&
Laura Ellen Anderson

from children's TV presenter
Cerrie Burnell
Ballet Dreams
Cerrie Burnell & Laura Ellen Anderson

From children's TV presenter
Cerrie Burnell
Fairy Magic
Cerrie Burnell
Laura Ellen Anderson

Also look out for . . .

HARPER AND THE Night Forest